A Man Walks Into A Hardware Store

Bernie Van De Yacht

A Man Walks Into A Hardware Store

By

Bernie Van De Yacht

For my beloved wife, Valerie, and my two sons, Janssen and Joseph.

"In sickness and in health, until death do us part."

Part One

Chapter One
He Had Already Left the Store

The tarnished shop bell's high-pitched tone signaled his entrance into her life, as well as into the antiquated hardware store where she'd worked for as long as she could remember.

Her first image of him was through the convex security mirror suspended over the "Nuts and Bolts" aisle. His face had a haunted look. It was eerily reminiscent of the lost potential and unforgiving harshness of a mug shot, yet there was residual evidence suggesting he hadn't always looked this way. There were the soulful brown eyes framed in long lashes, the full head of dark hair graying around the temples, and the cleft chin. She'd always had a thing for cleft chins.

She knew he wasn't from around these parts by the way he was dressed—conservative white-collar attire, pressed and creased in all the right places, just like you see in those men's fashion magazines that nobody buys. He was nothing like the cowboys in Porterville. They were just creased. And dusty. No, he was different, and she was intrigued by different. Different rarely entered her hardware store.

She hunched over the counter, watching him with a mixture of bemusement and pity. He was looking for something and she could easily help him. But that would spoil all the fun of waiting for him to ask. 'Cause she knew all men hated to ask.

He looked uneasy and restless as he wandered down aisle after aisle. She figured he did what most customers did—limited his gaze to the center of the shelves, not thinking to check the top and the bottom. She wasn't about to let him leave her store having made that common mistake.

Stubborn men, she thought. *Why can't they just admit it when they need help?*

"You look lost," she finally said. "Something I can help you with?"

"I'm fine, thanks," he replied. His voice had a pleasant quality. Kind and easy on the ear, if a little timid.

"Suit yourself. Been working here darn near my whole life and I've never had a man ask for help. Figured you might be different."

He stopped his search momentarily and looked at her. "Why would you think that?"

"'Cause you look more lost than most," she said, standing up straight, putting her hands on her waist and jutting out her breasts. She caught his eyes give her chest a quick glance, then he put his head down and began to make a beeline for the exit.

"I'm sorry. I don't think you have what I'm looking for."

"Bullshit." She came around the counter and hastily followed him to the door. "We've got everything the big stores got. Try me."

He stopped, took a deep breath, then slowly turned and said, "All right. Fire escape ladders. You know those things . . ."

"Yeah," she said, cutting him off. "I know what they are. Like I said, been working here since I was a kid." She began making her way down the third aisle. "Follow me."

She was halfway to the shelf before she realized he wasn't following. She turned around and glared at him with an impatient look on her face.

"Well, you coming or are you gonna just keep staring at my ass?"

His face turned bright red as he sputtered, "No-no. I wasn't." He was breathing heavily now.

"Sure you were. Wouldn't be normal if you didn't look. Even if you are 'married.' " She couldn't say "married" without sounding sarcastic. The word didn't sit well with her. She didn't believe in marriage because she'd never seen one work.

"How did you know I was married?"

"The wedding ring is a pretty good tip-off."

"Oh, yeah," he said, and then he began to twist his wedding ring around his finger. It appeared to calm him.

"Got kids?"

The man looked as though he didn't particularly like being probed about his personal affairs. "Just one. A girl."

"What's her name?"

The man didn't reply.

"I said . . ."

"Miranda," he said quickly. "Now can we just—I don't have a lot of time."

"Typical man. Wanna get right to it."

She resumed walking to the middle of the aisle and then crouched down and grabbed a red oblong box. "This one's the best," she said, handing him the box. "Got anti-slip rungs. It'd suck to slip and break your neck when you're trying to escape from a fire."

She walked to the front counter and hoisted herself up on top of it, not bothering to cross her legs. She'd given up acting "lady-like" years ago—it was way too much work. Besides, she was wearing jeans, so it didn't really matter. She'd cross them if she was wearing a dress, but she didn't own any so she didn't have to concern herself with that nonsense.

"So, what brings you here today?" she asked. "You could have gone to Home Depot, or as I like to call it, Home Despot, but you chose Hardware California."

He paused for a moment to think. Then he said, "I… ah… liked your sign."

He was referring to the retro neon sign hanging over the front entrance that had "Hardware California" written in a seventies-style cursive. It was turned on from the time they opened until the moment they closed. Even with the sun shining at high noon, you could see it lit up, blinking on and off like something you'd see at a cheap motel in Las Vegas.

"My dad designed that sign when he opened the store," she said. "He was so proud of it. My mom always thought it looked tacky and cheap. When he died, she wanted to bury it with him. But then we decided to cremate him, so the sign stayed. Love it or leave it, at least it draws you in."

The man looked around the store. There was no one else there. "Do you run the store by yourself now?"

"Basically. My mom helps out, but she's getting up there so I end up doing most of the work."

"A family business. Don't see much of those anymore."

"Yeah," she laughed. "There's a reason for that. But that's a topic for another day. Another time."

She jumped off the counter and walked over to him, only the ladder separating them.

"So, what do you think?"

He looked in her eyes for a fleeting moment, then quickly dropped his head and began to read the warning label on the box with the intensity of someone on a diet checking the calorie content of a candy bar. "How many you got?" he asked.

"Five," she replied without checking. "Including the one you're holding." She knew her inventory like ranchers know their horses. The first job her father ever gave her was managing and stocking the supply room. Back then, she loved organizing the shelves, making sure everything was in its place, and nothing ever ran out. But then one day she let it all go, and the room had been a mess ever since.

She realized a long time ago that things didn't need to be perfect in order to function.

"I'll take all of them."

"All of them?" she asked, surprised. "You don't need them in every room, ya know."

"I know," he replied.

She looked at him curiously. "Your house burn down or something?"

"It's just, my wife... she likes to feel safe."

"Typical woman," she scoffed. "Glad I ain't one of 'em."

"You're not a woman?"

"Funny. Yeah. I'm a woman," she said, leaning towards him, her breasts pressing into the box. "I'm just not typical."

She bent down, grabbed the other four boxes, and began making her way back to the counter. They were heavy as shit, but she sure wasn't about to ask the man for help.

"Let me help you with those," he said, trying to catch up with her.

"That's okay. I've got it," she said, dropping them on the counter, causing every window in the store to rattle. "You sure five will be enough? I can order more if you think your wife won't find five safe enough."

"Five is fine," he said, as he gently placed his box on the counter next to her stack. He reached into his back pocket and pulled out a wad of cash bound together by a thick rubber band.

"Good God! You gonna pay in cash?" she asked. "Don't tell me—your wife doesn't feel credit cards are safe, either?"

His look said it all. She kind of felt sorry for the guy.

"I remember the first time someone tried to buy something with a credit card. My dad 'bout had a fit. 'Cash or checks is all I'll ever accept at Hardware California,' he'd say. First thing I did when he died is put in a credit card machine. But, by then, it was too late. Most of our customers had gone off to Home Despot. Only the loyals are left. And people like you who stop in because something catches their eye—like a sign."

"So… how much do I owe you?" he said, as he removed the rubber band from his bundle of bills.

"With tax…" she said, punching the keys on an archaic National Cash Register. "Two hundred and ninety-eight dollars."

It was a lot of money, but she noticed that he didn't blink.

Must be loaded, she thought.

Funny, though, he didn't act like someone with money. That was a good thing. Men with money always acted entitled. And they were terrible in bed. They made love like they were doing you a favor. The ones just scraping by knew how to show their appreciation.

She watched him as he counted out the money. His hands were trembling. Might have a medical condition, she speculated. Or just plain nervous. Either way, she was intrigued by him.

"You just move here? I haven't seen you around town and I know damn near everybody."

"I keep to myself. I mean, we do. My family, that is," he said, without looking up, his voice barely above a whisper.

He laid his money on the counter, fanning it out like a winning hand of cards. "There. Two hundred and ninety-eight dollars."

She scooped up the money without counting it and put it in the register. Something about him told her he was trustworthy, even if he was acting a little strange. But strange didn't bother her. She'd never met a man who wasn't strange.

He grabbed three of the boxes and headed toward the door. "I'll come back for the others."

"Nonsense," she said, as she grabbed the other two. "No point in making two trips."

"Okay. Have it your way," he said, as he hurried for the door.

"I always do," she said, smiling.

But he didn't hear her. He had already left the store.

Chapter Two
I Can't Breathe

He drove a Volvo. Safest car on the road.

His wife must have picked it out, she thought. *No man would ever choose to drive a Volvo.*

She watched him from behind, as he stacked the boxes neatly in his trunk. He even took extra care to ensure that the labels were all facing the same way.

"You're so neat," she observed, amused. "The way you packed those boxes, I'm tempted to hire you to stock my shelves."

She gazed into the car. There was a child's booster chair in the back seat. It was spotless. No dried ketchup stains or crushed Cheerios in the crevices. Not even a melted crayon encrusted into the fabric. Hell, it looked like it'd never been used.

He slammed the trunk shut, then walked around to his door and opened it. "Well, I'd better get going."

"Wait," she said. "Do you wanna see mine?"

He looked at her inquisitively. "Your...?"

"My wheels."

He looked around uneasily. "I really have to go," he said, jingling his keys.

"C'mon. You showed me yours. Now I gotta show you mine. Wouldn't be fair."

He glanced at his watch for a moment and then replied. "Um, sure. I guess. But I have to make it quick."

"Most men do," she said, sardonically. "Follow me. And try not to look at my ass this time."

***

He began to follow her, trying to look everywhere but at her posterior. The afternoon sun illuminated her scarlet hair. Like a raging crimson river, it was untamed. Wild. It moved in sync with her curvaceous body. She walked with a self-assured gait that seemed purely organic and natural.

There was nothing phony about this woman, he thought.

She was, therefore, the complete opposite of him. He always felt so guarded, so self-conscious, so uncomfortable in his own skin. He wondered what she saw in him, or did she see anything? Perhaps she was this friendly and open with everyone and he wasn't anything special at all to her. She was probably just lonely and needed someone to talk to and he happened to be in the right place at the right time.

As they rounded the corner of the store, he saw a small red barn with a white fence in desperate need of a paint job. As the woman approached the fence, a sinewy chestnut horse with a white blaze running the length of its forehead emerged from the barn and trotted eagerly towards her. The woman buried her hands in its mane and pressed her lips on its forehead. The horse responded by placing its muzzle in the crick of her neck. The man turned away, embarrassed, yet captivated by their almost sensual interaction.

"My wheels," she said, as she stroked the horse's mane. "When my car blew its engine last year I said, 'Screw it. My horse can get me where I need to go just as good as a car.' So, whattaya think?"

He hesitated before answering. He felt uneasy around horses. Sure, they were beautiful creatures, but he preferred to admire them from afar, running in a field, or marvel at a photographer's image of them captured in the pages of a glossy coffee table book. He was uncomfortable being so close to the real thing. It was the way they looked at him with those dark, knowing eyes that could read his mind and see all his secrets.

The horse emitted a low-key, agitated breath that unnerved the man. It seemed to be trying to convey something to him and it wasn't friendly. The man found himself unable to breathe for a moment—as if the horse had sucked the air out of his lungs.

"She's beautiful," he finally managed.

"*He's* beautiful," she corrected him. "I'd never own a female. Too much drama."

"What's his name?" he asked.

"Stud-Muffin." And then, turning to him, she said, "And yours? Just dawned on me that I never got your name."

"Terry," he said. "Terry Boyle." He thought about extending his hand but decided against it. It seemed too formal. Who was he kidding? It seemed too intimate.

But then she extended hers. "I'm Renee Patrick."

He took her hand. It was softer than he'd imagined.

She cast her eyes downward, looking surprisingly vulnerable for the first time since they'd met, and then slipped her hand from his and turned to her horse. "Stud-Muffin here is the closest I'll ever get to being married."

"I wouldn't give up hope," he offered sympathetically. "You're—"

"Save it. I don't need your pity. I love men and they love me. Just don't want to marry one."

"Never?" Terry asked.

"Never," Renee replied resolutely, as she stroked Stud-Muffin's forelock.

After a moment of awkward silence, Terry said, "Well, I really need to get back to work."

"One of those bosses, huh?"

"Yeah."

Terry felt the urge to say more—to end their brief meeting with something other than, "yeah."

"Thanks for the ladders," he said. It was all he could come up with.

"No problem. Glad I had what you were looking for."

He nodded, then slowly turned away from her and began to walk to his car.

"Come back again sometime, Terry Boyle," Renee called after him.

Terry looked back and smiled. "Maybe I will." And then he disappeared around the corner.

***

After he was gone, Renee turned to Stud-Muffin. "Well, that went well, wouldn't you say?" Stud-Muffin cocked his head slightly to the side, as if to disagree.

"Too bad he'll never come back, though. 'Maybe' is the same as saying 'never.'"

***

Terry pulled off to the side of the road the moment the store was no longer visible in his rearview mirror. He was shaking so intensely, he could barely steady his hands to make the call to the one person who could soothe him.

"I need to see you right away," Terry gasped painfully, once the person finally answered. "I can't breathe."

Chapter Three
As If He'd Ever Forget

Terry snuggled next to Miranda on her frilly peppermint pink bedspread, reading a book aloud. He'd been reading the thick book to her for more than a month, but now they were on the last two sentences of the last page.

"And in a blinding flash, the sun returned to the sky. A new day had begun," he said, as he closed the book. "The End."

They lay there for a few moments without saying anything. Just absorbing the conclusion and feeling satisfied with how everything ended up working out. He liked books with happy endings.

Miranda eased the book from his hands and placed it on her nightstand. "Do you think I could read to you tomorrow, Daddy?"

He smiled every time she said "Daddy." It never got old. He dreaded the day she'd start calling him "Dad." Some girls never stopped saying "Daddy." Maybe, he hoped, she would be one of those girls.

He gave her a look of feigned hurt. "Don't you like the way I read to you?"

"Of course," she said. "But I want to show you how good I read. Mrs. Vespers said I'm one of the best in the class."

"I'll bet you are. It's just—I like reading to you. I've been doing it ever since you were a baby."

He hated to see her grow up. She was seven already and her eighth birthday was right around the corner.

Eight.

Eight seemed so much older than seven. Time was moving too fast. Before he knew it, she would be going off to college, where their relationship would be reduced to intermittent phone calls, occasional texts, brief holiday vacations, and, God forbid, Snapchat.

"But I'm not a baby anymore."

He looked at her sadly. "You'll always be my baby. No matter how old you get."

"Please, Daddy?" she pleaded with her sea blue eyes that always melted his resolve.

"Okay. I'll think about it," he said. This seemed to pacify her. Just like it did every night. Of course, they'd have the same conversation tomorrow.

"Good night, Daddy," she said.

"Good night, honey," he replied, as he planted a kiss on her soft cheek.

"Don't forget," she whispered, as he walked toward the door.

He turned back. She was staring at an empty vase next to the book on her nightstand. "I never do," he assured her. He switched off her light. It flickered a few times before it went out.

Gotta call an electrician about that, he thought. *Tomorrow. First thing.*

***

Terry's parents never read to him when he was Miranda's age. Or any age, for that matter. They were too busy fighting with each other. Eventually their fighting culminated in a divorce when he was eleven years old, and it irrevocably changed his life. Before their divorce, his parents fought constantly, but he'd grown used to it. It was all he knew. After they divorced, he became a helpless knot on the rope in the middle of his parents' never-ending game of tug-of-war. He was always being made to choose sides between the two of them. Ultimately, he chose neither of them and just checked out emotionally.

After graduating high school, Terry had no idea what to do for a job. All he knew was that he had to find something that paid enough to allow him to live on his own. He found his answer in the classified section of the *Antelope Valley Press*. It was an ad for a local insurance course that promised instant employment upon completion. He immediately enrolled in the program, passed the exam, and got his license. Within two weeks of getting his license, he was offered a job at a big insurance company in Burbank. It was his ticket out of Lancaster, but most importantly, away from his parents.

Working at a big company proved to be a mistake, though. There were too many people. All the concurrent conversations and constant commotion made him uneasy. He rarely talked to anyone unless he was forced to. He preferred to stay in his cubicle, hidden behind its protective gray fabric walls. He even kept a little refrigerator by his desk so he wouldn't have to go to the break room. Everyone was always gossiping or talking about some vapid reality show they'd seen on TV the night before. He hated small talk and was beginning to realize that he didn't really like people in general. He just wanted to be left alone.

But all that changed the day he met Hannah Loggins.

That fateful morning, his alarm failed to go off. It was a new clock radio and he couldn't quite figure out how to set it properly. He was never good at following instructions or learning how to operate new gadgets. As a result of his mishap, he overslept by a half hour. Therefore, his morning routine had to be truncated to compensate for the loss of time. In his haste, he neglected to grab the lunch he'd prepared the evening before, the same lunch he brought to work every day—a ham sandwich with a dab of Miracle Whip on rye bread, plain potato chips, a dill pickle wrapped in tinfoil, and a small bottle of water. If he drank too much water during the day, he'd have to pee, which meant he'd have to leave his cubicle more often. And possibly be forced into an uncomfortable conversation with someone in the urinal beside him. The mere thought of it made him break out in a sweat. So, a few sips of water during the day would suffice. He rarely finished the bottle.

By lunchtime, his stomach was growling so loudly his meddlesome partition-mate kept popping her head up and giving him dirty looks. He normally ate at his desk, but his hunger pangs were not subsiding, so he had no choice but to venture out of the office for lunch.

He thought about taking his car and going to a drive-thru, but parking was so limited in the lot that he'd probably not find an open spot when he returned. And driving in circles made him sick to his stomach. Puking at work was not an option. The only place within walking distance was the food court at a local mall. That's where everyone else went for lunch. He hoped he wouldn't run into any of his co-workers, and he especially hoped they wouldn't invite him to eat with them. He just wanted to get something quick and dash back to the office.

There were a lot of options in the food court, and too many choices frustrated him. After wasting fifteen minutes of his lunch hour trying to make up his mind, he finally settled on Subway. Partly because it had the shortest line. He ordered a ham sandwich with a dab of mayonnaise (they didn't offer Miracle Whip) on a French roll (ditto rye bread), and a bag of plain potato chips. He decided to forgo the pickle. They weren't the kind he liked. And no water.

On the way out of the mall, he took a shortcut through the big anchor store, Landers—his plastic Subway bag swishing back and forth as he hurried back to the safety of his partitioned fortress.

As he was passing the fragrance department, he unexpectedly felt something moist sprayed on the back of his neck. He stopped, wiped it off, and smelled it.

It smelled like tar. And rust.

He turned around, slightly irritated that he'd have to spend another portion of his lunch hour scrubbing the scent off, and that's when he saw her for the first time.

His irritation dissolved as fast as the image on a shaken Etch-a-Sketch. She bore a slight smile on her face that was friendly, yet mischievous. Terry couldn't stop looking at her. She was perfect. And that meant one thing —she was way out of his league. Her job was simply to hawk the latest men's cologne and he was just one of her test victims.

"So, do you want *A Knight to Remember*?" she asked.

"Excuse me?" he barely eked out.

"It's a new men's cologne we're testing. It's the hottest fragrance in Europe. What do you think?"

He couldn't think, much less speak. All he saw was a beautiful girl taking the time to talk to him. That was all the pitch he needed. "I'll buy it," he blurted out. Although he knew he'd never wear it. On what such an occasion would one want to smell like tar and rust?

"Really?" she said. She was clearly delighted. "That's great! You're my first customer of the day."

"I find that hard to believe," he said. And he did. How could anyone say no to this woman? He'd buy anything she was selling. Even if it smelled awful.

She placed her hand on the small of his back and led him over to the counter. He felt as though he were floating along beside her.

"I'm Hannah Loggins. And you are?"

"Terry Boyle," he said, barely feeling the marble floor beneath his feet.

During the transaction, she peppered him a barrage of questions: "Have you ever been to Europe?" (No.) "What kind of cologne do you normally wear?" (None.) "Do you work around here?" (Yes.) "What sign are you?" (Cancer.) "Do you believe in fate?" (No.) Normally so many personal questions would have bothered him, but not coming from her. Especially when she asked, "Are you seeing anyone?"

He dropped his Subway bag. *This has to be a dream*, he thought. *It is too good to be true.*

"No," he stammered, bending down to pick up his bag. "Not at the moment."

"Then how about we go on a date?"

He instantly felt woozy and leaned against the counter for support. It was a combination of the lack of food, the sickening smell oozing from the skin on the back of his neck, and the prospect of actually getting to go on a date with this angelic Hannah Loggins.

"Are you okay? Am I coming on too strong?" she asked.

"No. I mean, yes, I'd like very much to go on a date with you." He stopped to catch his breath, then continued. "When?"

"How about tonight? Are you available?"

"Yes," he replied a bit too eagerly. She didn't seem to be put off by his rapid response. She seemed to be charmed by it.

She reached behind the counter and handed him a card. "Here. My number's on there. Call me when you get off work."

He looked at the card but couldn't make out the number. His vision was blurry from the whirlwind of stimuli swirling around his brain.

And then she leaned in and whispered in his ear, "Just do me one favor? Don't wear that cologne you just bought. It smells like shit."

He laughed. It was the best waste of money he'd ever spent.

They didn't end up going on a date that night. Rather, they stayed up all night at her apartment, talking. Actually, she did most of the talking, but Terry didn't mind. He didn't like to talk about himself anyway.

After that night, they were inseparable. Hannah came into his life that day and changed it forever.

He proposed to her three months after their first encounter and they were married six months after that. After a two-week honeymoon in Europe, Terry transferred to a small insurance company in Bakersfield. There were a lot less people there and they were nicer. At least they seemed nicer. He'd never really given the people at Burbank a chance. He actually liked going to work, but going home was even better.

Hannah was always waiting for him at the door, the aroma of a home-cooked meal emanating from the kitchen behind her. She was a great cook and Terry would watch in amazement as she'd concoct a delectable meal without the aid of a recipe book. Sometimes she would let him taste whatever she was making by licking her finger. But not very often, because it always led to sex and then the dinner burned. Life was good. It was better than good; it was bliss. Terry was living a dream.

And then they had Miranda.

***

"Earthquake!" shrieked Hannah in the dead of night. She bolted out of bed, grabbed her smokes off the nightstand, torched one, then stood as still as a department store mannequin in the frame of the bathroom door, waiting for the shaking to subside.

"Terry?! Did you feel that?!"

"Feel what?" he asked groggily, his head buried beneath his pillow.

"That earthquake. Just now."

"No."

"Are you nuts? How could you not feel that? It was huge. I'm going to check the news."

She switched on the TV, which caused stark shards of light to puncture the darkness.

"Come back to bed," Terry said. "It was probably just a tremor."

But she didn't hear him. She was too preoccupied trying to find a station that was reporting the earthquake's magnitude.

Terry knew he wasn't going back to sleep now that Hannah had turned on the TV. She wouldn't shut it off until she knew every last detail about the tremor—the magnitude, the epicenter, the probability of it being a precursor to something much bigger. "I'm going to go check on Miranda," he said, throwing off his covers.

"You need to get some earthquake safety kits tomorrow," Hannah said as she frantically flipped channels. "That was just a warning. The 'Big One' is coming. I just know it."

***

Terry quietly pushed open Miranda's door and peered into her room. All was well. She seemed to have slept through it and nothing had fallen on her. Just as he was about to close the door, something caught his eye. On the nightstand next to the bed, her flower vase was lying on its side. It hadn't broken, but the water and the handful of fresh wildflowers he'd picked for her after putting her to bed, had spilled onto the floor.

He entered the room quickly and inserted the flowers back in the vase. It was nearly morning, and he didn't want her to wake up and think he'd forgotten the promise he made to her one spring nearly two years ago.

Hannah had had a bad day, like so many before. Miranda had just turned six, and when he put her to bed that night he noticed that the tension of living with Hannah's illness had really taken its toll on her. He could see it in her eyes. A look so heartbreaking it defied description.

He couldn't get to sleep that night, so he decided to take a walk.

As he strode along the side of the road, haunted by that look in Miranda's eyes, he found himself drawn to the sight of the wildflowers that blanketed the landscape. They were impossible to ignore. Every spring, California desert wildflowers blossomed there for a limited period of time— usually from early March until mid-May. That was on a good year. And this year was particularly good.

Miranda loved them all—the pulsating purple lupine, the billowy white snowdrops, the brilliant orange poppies—but her favorite were the pink cosmos.

He suddenly got an idea. He crouched down and carefully selected a variety of flowers from the abundant choice nature offered.

When he returned home, he found a vase in the cupboard, placed the flowers in it, and put the arrangement on Miranda's nightstand.

That night he slept on her floor. He wanted to see her expression when she woke up.

He awoke the next morning to the sound of a piercing squeal. He reflexively jumped up, thinking it was Hannah.

Miranda's back was to him. She was looking at the vase of flowers. As he positioned himself to see her face, he could see she was smiling. That *look* had left her eyes.

"Do you like them?" he asked, delighted at her reaction.

"Yes, Daddy, I love them. They're so pretty!" She stretched her arms up toward him and he leaned down and hugged her. Though he had hardly slept, he felt instantly refreshed.

So every spring after that, when the wildflowers were in bloom, he'd gather a fresh bouquet, put them in a vase, and set them on Miranda's nightstand. When they'd start to wilt, he'd replace them with a new assortment. It was a promise he'd made to her that day and he never broke it. Still, she liked to remind him every now and then.

As if he'd ever forget.

Chapter Four
A Living Hell

Hannah used to embrace life; not try to escape it. There was a time when she didn't wake up every morning wondering if she could make it through the day. She used to smile, and even laugh. But then it all changed.

She would never forget the day. No mother would. It was the day she gave birth to her daughter, Miranda. God, that was hard for her to admit—even to herself.

This wasn't supposed to happen. Mothers love their children. Sometimes more than their spouses, even. But once she gave birth, she had a hard time feeling any emotion, much less love. Not for her husband, her baby, nor herself.

When did it start? Where did it all go wrong? She used to be so happy—especially during the first two years of marriage to Terry. Ever since she laid eyes on him, she knew he was the one. Perhaps it was the fact that he bore a striking resemblance to her father. Or maybe it was that, even though he was strikingly handsome, he didn't seem to know it. In that way, too, he was much like her father.

The first thing she noticed was the way Terry walked, determined and focused, like he was on his way to something really important. She had been working as a perfume pusher for Landers in Burbank for more than nine months and she hated it. It wasn't the job she hated so much as the people. They were all catty, the men even worse than the women. She wanted to quit but she was saving up money for a trip to Europe. She had always dreamed of traveling abroad and she was close to reaching her goal. Just a few more paychecks and she could put in her two weeks' notice. And then she'd be out of there—traveling the world, meeting interesting people, and maybe falling in love.

But Terry changed all that. Once she saw him, she knew her life would never be the same.

He was shy and unassuming, almost like a little boy. A stammering boy-man. He was someone she wanted to take care of and dote on—much like she had with her father until he died prematurely at the age of fifty-six.

She still couldn't believe her father was gone. He had always been sick, but he'd always told her that one day he would get better. She believed him, but he only got worse.

She met Terry five years to the day after her father died, and she took that as a sign. And she didn't ignore signs. She believed in fate. They got married nine months later. They went to Europe for their honeymoon and then returned to the States to begin their new life together. And it was wonderful—almost too perfect.

And then they decided to have a baby. The pregnancy was normal. There was a little scare in the beginning, something didn't look right during one of the exams, but it was so insignificant that later she couldn't even recall what it was. She gained a little over twenty pounds—normal for someone as small in size as she was.

And she never experienced morning sickness. She had always hated throwing up. The last time she threw up was in high school when she drank for the first and last time. When she became pregnant, she willed herself not to throw up, and she never did. Her mind was very powerful—capable of making her well, as well as driving her into madness.

Terry didn't like the name, Miranda, at first. He said it sounded too old-fashioned, but she insisted on it. She had read Shakespeare's *The Tempest* in high school and fallen in love with the play, especially the character of Miranda. She related to the relationship Miranda shared with her father, Prospero. They had a bond that was unbreakable, but complicated, especially when Miranda fell in love with the character, Ferdinand. Hannah identified with Miranda and vowed that if she ever had a daughter, that would be her name.

So Miranda it was, despite Terry's objections. It would have been worse if they'd had a boy. Hannah wanted to name a boy Ferdinand.

She remembered holding Miranda for the first time. Her baby was seven pounds of malleable flesh that shifted every time she took a breath, and Hannah thought, *I am responsible for every breath this child takes*. It scared the hell out of her and she felt a fear envelop her that she had never experienced before.

All she wanted was for the nurse to take the baby from her. And for life to go back the way it was.

She knew about postpartum depression, but this came on so quickly that she knew it had to be something else. She feared it was what her father had had. All his life he struggled with anxiety and depression and it only seemed to get worse with the years. Nothing seemed to help him—not therapy, not medication, not drinking. Nothing. He lived in misery until the day he died, when he just went to bed one night and never woke up again. His body and mind couldn't take one more day of the relentless anxiety.

She often wondered if she would die in the same way.

She never told Terry about her father's sickness. Her father had died before she met Terry, so she kept the details to herself. She didn't want Terry thinking she could inherit it. Besides, nothing in her disposition suggested she could possibly have a congenital mental illness. She was active, fun loving, and lived life to the fullest.

But when Miranda was born, illness crept in like a rising tide and pulled her out to sea. Nature had sucked her into the eye of a tempest.

She told Terry it wouldn't last and that she would beat it. At first, he was a big help—perhaps too big, because the more he did for her, the more she felt incapable of handling anything. She was terrified to hold Miranda. She would pick her up, but then quickly set her down so she didn't drop her or accidentally smother her. She couldn't bear the thought of anything happening to her, so she refused to put herself in a position where she might cause something to happen. She didn't trust herself. So she let Terry do everything.

But then she began to resent him. He seemed to do just fine without any help from her. There was no use in trying to get him to understand her condition, because he never would. His parents had divorced, but that wasn't the same. Divorce was something that happened to you. Mental illness happened within you.

She finally understood the pain her father had endured every day for his entire life.

Her life had become like his had been. A living hell.

Chapter Five
Won't Be the Last

The bell over the door of Hardware California chimed, signaling the arrival of a new customer. Renee looked up from the cash register, expecting one of her regulars, but it was Terry.

Huh, I was wrong, she thought. *"Maybe" doesn't always mean "never."*

"He came back, Mama! We're gonna have a good old-fashioned Irish wedding!" she shouted in the direction of the back office. Before Terry could protest, she said, "Relax. It's a joke."

"I knew that," he said, but he didn't sound convincing.

He's a terrible liar, she thought. *He has to be a faithful husband. His wife would be able to see it in his eyes.* "So, what brings you back this time? Besides me, of course."

"I need to buy some earthquake preparedness kits."

"Why? Are you expecting the big one?"

"Nothing wrong with being prepared. Just in case."

"Yeah, well. I always say, 'When it's my time to go, it's my time to go.'"

"Preparation saves lives," he said, sounding like an instructor at an earthquake preparedness symposium.

"Yes, sir. If you say so." She came around to the front of the counter. "C'mon. Let me show you our earthquake section. It's right next to the nuclear fallout supplies in case you're thinking of building an underground bunker."

As they were heading down the aisle, Renee's mother, Lois, appeared from around the corner. She was a round woman with a soft, puffy face that looked like it got stung by something and hadn't gone down yet. She lurked closely behind them, desperate to meet a patron who wasn't a regular.

"I'm with a customer, Mother," Renee said, her tone subtly suggesting her mother take a hike.

Lois reached for her glasses that were attached to a cheap crystal chain around her neck and brought them to her eyes. She gave Terry a slow once-over. "You the man that was in here the other day?" she asked. "I heard you from the supply room."

Lois took his hand in hers. "Lois Patrick," she said, with a girlish lilt.

"I'm Terry Boyle. You must be Renee's mother."

"Let go, Mom," Renee said after an uncomfortable moment. Turning to Terry, she added, "It's been a long time since she's touched a man."

Lois shot Renee a steely-eyed look before releasing Terry's hand. "We're glad you came back. Repeat customers are the reason we've been in business for over forty years."

"That, and your charming personality," Renee added dryly.

"Shut the hell up, you," Lois grumbled, before grabbing a bulky pleather purse from under the counter. "I'm off for a few hours. Anyone asks, I'm doing errands."

"Don't let her fool ya. She's going for her crystal meth fix."

Lois swatted Renee with her purse and then left the store, triggering the bell, which reverberated through the store.

Renee folded her arms and smiled at Terry. "So, you met my mother. Now it's official."

"Yeah, I know," he said. "Another joke."

Just then, the bell over the door rang again.

"What'd ya do? Forget your crack pipe?" Renee called out to Lois.

But it wasn't Lois. It was a wafer-thin woman with a pinched, angry look on her face. She stomped up to Renee and without hesitating, slapped her hard across the face. "Slut!" the woman seethed.

Renee made no attempt to defend herself, or even retaliate. In fact, she barely responded. It was almost like she was expecting it.

Impulsively, Terry took a step toward the woman, but Renee stopped him. "Don't," she said firmly, as a bright red handprint began to emerge on her cheek.

"You come near my husband again," she said, pointing a perfectly manicured finger in Renee's face. "I'll fuckin' kill ya." And then she pivoted on the heels of her pumps and stormed out, her pungent perfume lingering in the air like gun powder.

Renee put her hand on her cheek, and winced.

"That was the sheriff's wife. No one blames the man; they just take it out on me. Not the first time. Won't be the last."

Chapter Six
Unless You Want Me To, Of Course

"Want me to get you some ice?" Terry asked, shaken by what he'd witnessed. He didn't like standing idly by while someone he cared for was hurt. He felt helpless. And it brought up memories he wasn't prepared to revisit.

"There's a fridge in my office. But I can get it. She didn't break my legs," Renee said, as she walked down the hallway with her hand cupped over her swollen cheek.

"Want me to wait out here in case a customer comes in?" he called after her.

"I wouldn't if I were you. She may come back with a gun," she said, as she disappeared into her office.

Terry swung his head around and looked toward the entrance. "Are you kidding again?"

"Wouldn't put anything past a woman scorned," she called out. "Besides, she's married to a man who has lots of guns at his disposal."

In moments, he was standing in her doorway, breathing nervously. Renee was getting a bag of ice from a small fridge behind her desk.

Terry looked around the office, which had a masculine, lived-in feel. Thick, gold-colored drapes with yellowed backings hung from the only window. Beneath the window, a worn sofa had grease-stained throw pillows tucked in each corner. The walls were covered floor-to-ceiling with the type of dark paneling popular in the early '70s. Hanging haphazardly on the walls were a half-dozen framed pictures of horses, pulled from the pages of a magazine. They appeared to be strategically placed in random places, most likely to hide something unsightly.

"Sit down," she said, as she applied the ice pack to her swelling face.

He slowly began to move toward the sofa.

"Not there," Renee said quickly, as she set the ice pack on her desk. She went to a rickety, wooden chair and placed it in front of him.

"Here."

He looked at the chair. There was a stack of manila folders on it.

"Do you want me to take the folders off?"

"No. It'll be more comfortable with them on it."

Of the two, Terry thought the sofa would be the more comfortable, but he didn't question why she offered the chair instead. Perhaps she didn't want him to be comfortable.

"Sit," she said, as she reapplied the ice pack on her face. "Relax."

He shifted in his chair. It creaked loudly. "You didn't deserve that, you know," he said.

"Who're you foolin'? Course I did."

"No, you didn't," he insisted. "No one has the right to hit anyone else. That's what I tell Miranda."

"She's a child. I'm an adult. I can take it. Believe me, if I didn't think it was justified, I would have unleashed my Irish temper on her."

He looked at her inquisitively. "So… is it true? Did you sleep with her husband?"

"Many times."

He was shocked by her frank response. "Why?"

"Because he's a great lay."

"But he's married."

"I don't discriminate," Renee said, shrugging her shoulders. "Actually, I prefer singles, but it's a small town. I ran out of those a long time ago."

"And that doesn't bother you?"

"Not if it doesn't bother them. Takes two to tango, ya know."

"I know. I know. It's just…"

She pushed herself away from her desk and walked over to him. "Just what? Are you judging me?"

"No… I just don't understand." He looked up at her and shifted in his chair again. Another creak. It took all his might to sit still. He didn't know how many more creaks it could take before it all came crashing down beneath him.

"Don't try to understand me. You never will."

Renee backed up and stared at Terry inquisitively.

"Ya know, I've never met anyone like you," she said. "At least not around here."

"Am I that different?" he asked. Did she think he was some sort of freak?

"Yeah. For starters, most men love hardware stores. They walk in here like randy teenagers in an adult bookstore. But when you came in here yesterday, it was like the first time you ever stepped foot in one."

"Sorry to break it to you, but you weren't my first," he said, proud of himself for his clever use of double entendre. Renee smiled. She got the joke. "I just don't like them," he went on. "I try to avoid them if at all possible."

"So, why now? Why two days in a row? Am I really that good?"

Terry knew where she was going with this and he began to feel extremely uncomfortable. Rather than shifting in his chair again, he quickly stood up and walked over to the door. "This has to stop," he said, his back turned to her.

"What has to stop?"

"This. The way we're talking. It's not right. This kind of talk leads to things."

"Not unless you let it. Takes two to tango, remember?"

He didn't know what to say. All he knew was that he couldn't be her tango partner. Finally he said, simply, "Can you show me your earthquake preparedness kits now?"

"This wife of yours," Renee said, laughing. "I gotta meet her."

Terry spun around, his face chalk white. "I don't think that'd be a good idea. She doesn't have a very good sense of humor."

"Relax. I didn't mean that literally." Renee removed the ice pack from her face. "So, is she the one who sent you back here today?"

"No."

"I don't believe you. You know, being prepared is one thing. Getting yourself so worked up you can't function is another. Just live your life. Sometimes it's wonderful and sometimes… you get slapped in the face." She tapped at her puffy cheek. "By the way, how does it look?"

He examined her cheek from across the room. "I'd leave the ice on a little longer."

"Screw it," she said, and then put the ice pack back in the fridge. "I'm not planning on entering any beauty pageants." She kicked the door of the fridge shut and extended her hand toward him. "C'mon. Let me show you our earthquake kits. But I've got to warn you. They're probably covered in dust."

"I'll follow you," he said, but didn't take her hand.

"I don't bite, ya know," she said, as she slowly brushed past him. "Unless you want me to, of course."

Chapter Seven
Anything To Keep His Job

The embossed nameplate on the outside of Terry's door at Wayne Boydston Insurance Services was slowly succumbing to the forces of gravity. One good slam was all it would take to divorce it from its adhesive.

A series of sales awards displayed side by side in rows of four hung on the first visible wall as you entered his office. Terry put them there on purpose to impress his clients and his boss that he excelled at his job. All of the frames matched. There were eight in all, the most recent one awarded four years ago. There were a few more in a box under his desk, but he'd decided not to hang them. Too many would come off as boastful. Eight was just the right amount.

Behind his desk was suspended an oversized bulletin board that housed a smattering of Post-it notes and a season-themed calendar that was a month behind. Terry hadn't bothered to flip to the current month because he liked the vibrant photo featuring a field of wildflowers. They looked like the ones he picked for Miranda during spring's blooming season.

He sat behind his desk and began his day the way he always did—by staring at Miranda's most recent school picture, ensconced in a frame that still had the price tag glued to the glass. He hated it when retailers did that. No matter how hard he tried to get them off, he always ended up scratching the glass or breaking it. It was almost as if they did it on purpose to tick people off. He vowed to himself that today he would remove that sticker once and for all. He was tired of seeing even a portion of Miranda's image obscured by the handiwork of an overzealous price tagger.

Next to the picture of Miranda, there was a photo of Terry and Hannah on the beach in Newport. Tanned. Smiling. It was taken right before Hannah became pregnant with Miranda and it was the last great picture of the two of them. Hannah loved to run on the beach and soak up the sun's rays on the sand, but she never went near the water. She told him she didn't like the ocean. When he asked her why, she said she didn't know, she just didn't like it. She never elaborated. Terry thought that odd. He'd never met anyone who was afraid of the ocean. Even the shallow parts. It was the first time Hannah had revealed something about herself that clashed with her fearless personality. He'd shrugged it off at the time, but now he realized that her revelation was just the precursor to many irrational fears that would follow.

Letting out a heavy sigh, he turned on his prehistoric computer, sat back, and waited for it to chug to life at its usual glacial pace.

From outside his office, he heard heavy footsteps barreling down the hall toward his door. No one in the office moved quickly this early in the morning so he knew instantly that something was amiss. He craned his head toward the door and saw one of his co-workers, Kevin, a portly man in his late 40s, standing in the hall, panting.

"Can I come in?" he asked, his voice quivering. Kevin had the ruddy complexion of a chronic alcoholic even though he was a teetotaler, and was always sweating even though he never did anything even slightly strenuous.

"Of course. What's up?"

"Did you hear?"

"Hear what?"

"Boydston let Rick go," he said, dissolving into a chair in front of Terry's desk.

The news didn't surprise Terry. The agency was struggling and he had sensed for some time that someone had to go. He had just hoped it wouldn't be him. God knows what would happen if he lost his job.

"Who told you that?"

"Karen," he said.

Karen was the company's secretary and she knew things before anyone else did because she was consumed with everyone else's life but her own. And she reveled in salacious gossip. There was a look of pure glee on her face when she announced that Michael Jackson had died. Or Amy Winehouse. Or Heath Ledger. Or Prince. Or any other celebrity whose premature death would raise eyebrows and sell newspapers. She was striving for attention, and receiving a visceral reaction from someone filled that void. She didn't talk much about her life outside the office, and Terry assumed that she didn't have one. This job was her life.

"Are you sure?"

"I just walked by his office. He's packing it up. I didn't have the heart to stick my head in. He's been here longer than both of us."

"Got paid more, too. That's probably the reason they're getting rid of him," Terry surmised.

"You and I make the same," said Kevin. "Wonder which one of us will be next?" Kevin didn't know this, but Terry made more money than he did. A lot more. Karen told him. It was a secret he vowed to her he'd keep, and he was good at keeping secrets.

"I wouldn't worry about that," Terry said, trying his best to sound confident. "Someone's got to do the work around here and it sure isn't going to be Boydston. When would he have time to golf?"

Kevin took a labored breath. "I'm not worried. Jesus will provide. Matthew 6:27 says, 'Can any of you by worrying add a single moment to your lifespan?' " he recited.

For a man with such strong Christian convictions, he certainly didn't look content. In fact, he looked like he was about to implode.

Terry was concerned, too, but he concealed his feelings from Kevin. He was an expert at camouflaging his emotions. It was a talent he had perfected over the years.

Terry thought about the box of framed awards under his desk. Perhaps it was time to hang them. Show Boydston how valuable he was to the company.

Anything to keep his job.

Chapter Eight
Children Were So Good At Masking

"Looks like you're becoming a regular," Lois said when she saw Terry come into the hardware store. "Something I can help you find?"

"I was wondering… if Renee was here."

Lois eyed him suspiciously. "That why you come back?"

"No. It's not the only reason. I want to buy something."

"In that case, I can help you just as well as she could. What you looking for?"

"Actually, I was wondering if I could talk to Renee."

"I see," said Lois. "Talk? Is that all you want to do?"

"I don't know what you're insinuating," Terry said, displaying his wedding ring, "but I'm married."

"Most of 'em are," she said before she returned to adding up the few receipts the store had generated that morning.

"So, is she here?" he asked, a bit impatiently this time.

"Out back. Tending her horse."

***

As Terry rounded the corner of the store, he saw Renee inside the corral brushing Stud-Muffin with a rubber curry comb.

She glanced up at him when she heard him approach and then resumed grooming her horse. "What's it this time? 'Fraid we don't sell Uzis."

Terry noticed her tight-fitting, well-worn Western shirt. It was unbuttoned down to her cleavage.

"I can come back if you're busy."

"Never too busy for you. What you got?"

He held out the framed picture of Miranda. "I was wondering if you have anything to take this sticker off?"

She put the comb down on a weathered wooden bench next to Stud-Muffin's trough, and took the frame from him. Stud-Muffin glared at Terry intensely and then jerked his head away and trotted toward the barn, his tail swishing vigorously back and forth as if swatting away at a relentless fly.

"Don't you hate it when stores do that? Like they just want to piss you off."

"That's exactly how I feel," he said, as he watched Stud-Muffin staring at him from the confines of the stable—his steely eyes piercing from behind the swath of shadow cast by the partially open barn door.

She stared at the picture for a moment before asking, "This Miranda?"

"Yes," he said. It was strange to hear Renee say her name. He began to regret showing the picture to her.

"Got a lot of your features."

He nodded, but said nothing.

"Goo Gone'll do it. Got some in the store."

"Great. I'll buy it."

Renee continued to stare at the photo, and then placed it on the bench next to the curry comb.

"So. How's she handling it?" she asked, as she removed her grooming gloves.

"Who?"

"Miranda."

"How's she handling what?"

"The nutcase," Renee said.

Terry stiffened. "Are you referring to Hannah?"

"Oh, is that her name? Funny, you never mentioned it."

"My wife is not a nutcase," he said through clenched teeth. "She's a wonderful mother."

"And wife?"

"Yes. And wife."

"If you say so."

Terry could feel his anger rising and his throat constricting. It was a mistake to have come back. Why was she doing this? Why did she have to be so blunt and insensitive? "My wife isn't... well. But that doesn't mean that I don't love her or would ever think of leaving her. How would you like it if you got sick and your husband left you?"

"Well, I guess I don't have to worry about that since I'm never getting married."

He felt his chest tighten and he was beginning to feel panicky again. He had to get out of there. Fast. "You know, I think I'm going to leave."

Renee laughed. She thought he was kidding. But then he turned to go.

"Stop being so dramatic. I'm just messing with you. Don't get so worked up."

But he kept walking.

"Are you serious? Come back. What about your Goo Gone?"

"I'm sure Home Depot sells it," he called back to her. He quickly got in his car and raced out of the parking lot.

***

"Come back out, boy," Renee called to Stud-Muffin, who trotted towards her with an eager gait. "I think you're right about that one. Something's off about him."

As she reached for her gloves, she realized that Terry had forgotten Miranda's picture.

He'll be back, she thought.

Next time, though, she wasn't going to play nice. This one was going to be more work than the others. But, eventually, she'd break him. Just like all the others.

She picked up Miranda's picture and stared at it.

Great smile, she thought.

Children were so good at masking.

Chapter Nine
He Was Becoming a Regular

No bell rang when Terry stepped through the automatic doors of Home Depot. Of course if one had, he wouldn't have heard it over the frenzied, deafening activity occurring before his eyes like time-lapse photography.

Terry hated Home Depot. Everyone always seemed to know what they were there for and where to find it, except him. He was always reduced to asking some harried employee for help and he always had to describe it because he never knew its technical name.

"You know, those things that are made of steel and bent at an angle," he once struggled to explain to a clerk who couldn't care less. As if he was supposed to know that they're called Allen wrenches.

On a couple of occasions, he barely escaped being run over by a cart with swirling orange lights on top, driven by some teenager still stoned from a party he'd attended the previous night.

But this time was different. This time, he was armed. He had a name—Goo Gone. How hard could it be to find?

He began to wander the aisles, shifting his head from side to side, hoping he'd luck out and find it in one of the first few rows he ventured down. After trekking down six of them as long as football fields, he realized that he had to ask for help. It never failed.

Finding a clerk proved to be just as elusive as finding the damn Goo Gone. He finally spotted a lanky teenager with pimply skin lumbering toward him in a

Home Depot vest. From three yards away, he noticed his neck was covered in raw hickies. It was obvious he was proud of them, for he made no attempt to cover them up. In his day, kids went to great lengths to hide their hickies, even if it meant wearing a turtleneck in the middle of July. They were a sure sign to your parents that you were "doing it." If a girl was sucking on your neck, it was most likely not the only thing she was sucking. Nowadays though, it didn't seem like anyone cared—apparently not his parents, nor the managers of Home Depot.

God, he *was* getting old. He was even saying "nowadays."

"Excuse me?" he said to the kid as he breezed right by him. "Excuse me?" he repeated, a bit louder the second time.

"I'm on my break," said the kid, the velocity of his stride increasing the closer he got to the "Employees Only" door.

"This will be quick, I swear."

The kid turned around and looked at him with droopy, blood-shot eyes. "What?"

"I'm looking for your Goo Gone."

The kid shook his head, turned away. "It's right on the shelf behind you. Jesus, look next time before you ask."

He turned around. Sure enough. Goo Gone, as far as the eye could see.

***

It wasn't until he closed his car door shut and placed the bag on the empty passenger seat that Terry realized he'd left Miranda's picture at the hardware store.

Now he'd have to go back. And face Renee again.

Lois was right. He was becoming a regular.

Chapter Ten
He Was More Determined Than Ever

Terry placed his arm around the passenger side headrest, swiveled his head around, and accelerated as he looked out the back window of his car. Miranda was in her booster seat, gazing out the window. He glanced at his watch. They were on time for once, even a little bit early. Something told him today was going to be a good day.

And then he heard the scream.

"*Stop!*"

The potential for a good day had just been derailed.

He slammed on the brakes and glared at Hannah through the windshield. She stood unsteadily on the edge of the threshold that designated where the safety of the house ended and the uncertainty of the outside world began.

"I didn't see you put Miranda's seat belt on!"

Miranda stuck her head out of the window and called out, "I did it myself, Mommy."

Hannah furrowed her brow, unconvinced. "When did you learn how to do that?"

"A long time ago," she answered. "When I was a kid."

"Are you sure it's secure?"

"Yes, Mommy. I heard it click."

"Okay, then," Hannah said, nodding her head slowly. "As long as you heard it click." Reassured, but still disconcerted, she slowly closed the door to the outside world.

As Terry began to back out of the driveway again, he caught the look on Miranda's face. She looked deflated.

"You okay, honey?" he asked, as he turned onto the road.

Miranda looked at Terry's face in the rearview mirror. "What's wrong with Mommy?"

"Nothing," he answered. He could see that she wasn't buying it. "She'll be fine. She's just worried about you."

"She's worried about everything."

He knew it was his job to reassure his daughter, assuage her fears and doubts, but it was impossible when everything she was saying was true.

"She'll get better one day," he said. He'd been telling this to Miranda for years, but she was clearly losing hope that that day would ever come.

"You're not going to divorce her, are you?"

He shot a glance at her in the mirror. Miranda was staring down at her pink Hello Kitty backpack.

"Of course not, honey. Why would you ask that?"

"Because if you get a divorce, I'll kill myself."

Terry immediately jerked the steering wheel to the right and pulled the car over to the side of the road. He removed his seat belt so he could turn to face her.

"What would make you say something like that?" he asked, barely able to disguise the panic in his voice.

"Mommy. She says it all the time."

He looked directly into her eyes. "I will never divorce your mother. We are a family. We may not be perfect, but no family is. We're just going through some rough times. But when I married Mommy, it was for good times and bad. She will get better, I promise you. And someday, we will all live happily ever after. Just like in the fairy tales."

She looked at him with disillusion in her eyes. "I don't believe in fairy tales anymore, Daddy."

Terry's heart sank. She had been robbed of her sense of innocence by Hannah.

This couldn't go on; something had to change. Maybe not today, and maybe not tomorrow, but he was determined to do something. Something he'd been thinking about doing for a long time but lacked the courage to carry out. But now he was determined.

He was more determined than ever.

Chapter Eleven
Before It Was Too Late

Renee really wasn't in the mood for sex this early in the day, but the man had a limited window of time so she had to take it or leave it. Besides, he had to get back to work so he could provide for his wife and kids. He was a devoted family man, after all.

He wasn't the best lay she'd ever had, but he was better than most. He was not very attractive, but his sexual performance made up for all he lacked. As the years eroded away, she became less and less particular about things that used to matter, like physical appearance. That was the first to go. Then, age—as long as he was alive, he was fair game. From the beginning, marital status had never mattered. Hell, she was doing it with married men when she was still in high school. Some of them were even teachers. They taught her, all right.

There was one character flaw she refused to allow, though, and that was abusiveness. She couldn't stand sadistic assholes. There would be none of this crazy masochistic talk, or hair pulling, or slapping in any way, shape, or form. One unfortunate fellow tried that, and she kicked him in the balls so hard that he nearly fainted. He was never invited back in again.

Most of the time it was in their cars. She lost count of how many times she'd had to wait in the front seat while the man struggled to remove a baby seat so they could be more comfortable in the back. Or help him put Christmas gifts he'd just bought his wife in the trunk so they wouldn't get squished. When they were done, they'd both go to work ensuring there was no evidence of their transgression—like criminals cleaning up after a crime. Everything was put back in place and no one was the wiser.

Motels were the best, but most of her lays were too cheap to shell out the money. Plus, they didn't want their rendezvous to be traceable by credit card. She never charged them—that would make her a prostitute, something she was not. But she did wish that some of the time they would at least spring for a room with a shower so she could wash away the smell of sex when they'd finished. She hated coming back to the store after one of her car encounters and be forced to endure the *look* her mother would give her.

Renee was growing impatient because this one was taking longer than usual. With her hands gripped around him tightly, she could feel the coarse gray hair on his fleshy back beneath her fingernails. The strands were sweaty, but taut. No amount of moisture could change their consistency. Gray hair was the most stubborn follicle on earth.

She just wanted him to finish, but his little blue pill was allowing him to continue on like a man half his age. She had work to do back at the hardware store. Supplies had to be ordered and she had a pile of bills to pay. Plus, her mother would be wondering where she was, even though she'd have a pretty good idea.

And Terry might return to pick up his picture and she'd miss him. She couldn't get him out of her mind. She knew it was just a matter of time before he caved. All men did.

With one final thrust, he finished.

"That was great," she said with a practiced conviction. Truth be told, it wasn't that great. She'd derived more pleasure cleaning out her ear with a Q-tip.

"The best," he managed breathlessly, his entire body convulsing with a series of mild internal aftershocks. He smiled like a stupid teenager as he pulled up his pants and tightened his snakeskin belt.

As she sat up, she caught sight of her face in his rearview mirror, and it was one she hardly recognized. *Who is that wretched woman?* she thought.

She looked over at him. He was still smiling. *Why was he so happy? Was he going to go back to work and tell his co-workers what he'd done? Was he going to make love to his wife tonight and think of her? Couldn't he just get off in the shower like most men? Why did he need her?* And then she wondered, *Why did I need him?*

He leaned in to kiss her, but she avoided it by pretending to struggle with a stubborn button on her blouse. She hoped he wouldn't try again, because she had an uncontrollable urge to slap him across the face. Or vomit. This wasn't fun anymore. In fact, it stopped being fun a long time ago. Lately, it felt more like an addiction.

They drove back to the hardware store in silence, that silly smile still plastered across his stupid face. She turned away in disgust and stared out the window at the multi-colored wildflowers alongside the road. She needed to see something beautiful to compensate for the ugly way she felt inside.

When would it end? Someday she'd lose her appeal to men—and then what? Someday she'd look like her mother; be like her mother. Alone. Bitter.

Something had to change. Her life couldn't continue on like this. She had to do something drastic.

Before it was too late.

Chapter Twelve
For Miranda's Sake

Miranda and her classmates had all been instructed by the elementary school staff that the monkey bars on the other side of the playground were strictly off-limits because they were not designed to meet today's safety standards. But that only intrigued Miranda more. The new playground equipment they installed over the summer was for babies. It lacked challenge, and Miranda liked a good challenge.

Each recess, she would wait patiently until the teachers were looking the other way, and then she'd climb through the hedge separating the old playground from the new one, and play alone and unhindered on the monkey bars until lunch hour was over. Most days she got away with it.

But not this day. Once the shrill whistle rang out over the schoolyard, she knew she'd been busted.

She carefully began to descend the metal rungs, prolonging the inevitable consequences that would surely greet her at the bottom. She looked down and sure enough, there was Mr. Quayle, the vice-principal, waiting to dole out her punishment. She smiled at him innocently and shrugged her shoulders. He didn't smile back.

When she was halfway down, her sneaker slipped on a rusty bar and she lost her footing. She made a desperate attempt to grab something for support, but all she managed to catch was air. So down she went, hitting every bar along the way on her plummet to earth.

She landed hard on the blacktop, her arm cushioning her fall. At first she thought she was okay, but then the pain hit her and Mr. Quayle became all blurry.

***

"I'll be right there," Terry said, anxiously into the phone. "Can you meet me?"

"*No! I can't meet you! You know that!*" Hannah screamed in reply.

He quickly closed his office door, convinced that her screech could be heard through the receiver.

Hannah paced back and forth like a caged animal as she inhaled short, nervous drags from her cigarette.

"*Go and get her now!*" she demanded. "Soon as that cast is on, I want her home safe with me."

Safe with her, he thought to himself. *How ironic*.

***

Hannah was waiting at the door when Terry and Miranda got home from the hospital.

"Where's her cast? I thought they said it was broken," Hannah said, when she saw Miranda's arm in a sling.

"It was just a sprain," he explained in a calm voice. "She's fine." He didn't want Hannah to freak out Miranda more than she already was.

"Are you sure? Did they take X-rays?"

"I think they can tell the difference between a sprain and a break."

Miranda stood between them, looking up, absorbing every word.

"She could have landed on her head," fumed Hannah. "This happens again, I swear she's not going back to school. Wasn't anyone watching her?"

Miranda looked at her father, her eyes pleading for him not to tell.

"It was an accident," he said. "Plain and simple."

"Go in the bathroom, Miranda," instructed Hannah. "I'll be right there. We need to clean you up. Hospitals are full of sick germs."

Miranda hung her head and walked dutifully to the bathroom.

"It's those Goddamned monkey bars. Someone probably gets hurt every day and they just cover it up," Hannah said. "I should sue their asses."

"Can you tone it down a notch? This was very traumatic for her."

"And it wasn't for me?"

"If you were so concerned, you would have…"

"Don't even go there with me. Not today. My nerves are fried."

He dug in his pocket and pulled out his keys.

"Where are you going?" she asked.

"Back to work," he said.

"Can't you stay home for the rest of the day? Miranda needs you."

"No, I can't," he said firmly. "They just fired Rick. Kevin and I are taking on all his clients. I'm doing double the work now."

"When did they fire Rick?" she asked, anxiously.

"Last week."

"Why didn't you tell me?"

"Because I thought it would upset you."

"Damn right it upsets me. What if you're next? If you lose your job, we're screwed."

"That's why I have to get back to work. So I don't lose my job," he said in a measured manner, as if he were talking to a child.

She spun away from him. "I want you to take down the swing in the backyard tonight when you get home."

"What? Miranda loves it."

"When she was four, she did. She hasn't been on it in years. I've always hated that thing. I'd rather have her play inside on the computer or something. She can't get hurt that way."

"Shouldn't we ask Miranda?"

"I want it gone in the morning," she said, and then continued on her way.

Keep it in, he told himself. *For Miranda's sake.*

Chapter Thirteen
But Wayne Never Turned Back Around

Terry pecked away at his well-worn keypad, inputting numbers to a computer program in a noble effort to find a better automobile insurance rate for Gloria Pickens—a loyal client for nearly a decade who, like most of his clients, had fallen on hard times. He knew he couldn't do anything better than what her present policy provided, but she was sitting in front of him with expectant eyes and he had promised her he'd try.

Everyone these days was trying to cut back and get a better rate. Making mortgage payments and putting food on the table were at the top of people's lists of priorities. Full coverage insurance was becoming a luxury that more and more people were deciding they could live without. They just wanted the minimum required by law. They'd take their chances, they told him, hoping nothing catastrophic would ever befall them.

He was not that confident. He had been an insurance salesman for most of his adult life and he knew better. He'd seen accidents shatter perfect lives firsthand and on a daily basis. He wasn't going to take his chances. Not with a wife like Hannah. She was worth every penny he doled out each month on the premium for her million-dollar life insurance policy.

Suddenly there was a loud rap on the door. He knew it was his boss, Wayne Boydston, by the way he knocked— boldly and authoritatively. Gloria almost jumped out of her skin. Terry barely moved. He was used to it after all these years.

Wayne was a few years older than Terry, but he was in far better shape. That's what going to the gym five days a week will get you. Terry had never been to a gym. Besides, even if he wanted to go, he didn't have the time. He was too busy taking care of a dysfunctional household and trying to hold on to his job.

"Can I see you in my office," said Wayne. It was not a question, but a statement.

"Now?" he asked. "I haven't quite finished up with Gloria."

Wayne left without replying. Either he didn't hear him or didn't care.

Terry looked at Gloria sympathetically. "Don't worry, Gloria. I'll get you a better rate. My boss can wait."

"Nonsense," said Gloria. She gathered up her papers and stuck them in a manila envelope marked "Assurance Needs." Terry couldn't decide if she had misspelled the word "insurance" intentionally or not. He was too polite to ask and, besides, it basically meant the same thing.

"You gotta jump when the boss calls," she said. "No one can afford to lose their job in times like these."

***

When Terry first started working for Wayne Boydston Insurance Services, there was no *Wayne* at the beginning of the company's name. It was simply Boydston Insurance Services. Terry liked Wayne's father, Walter, but he never cared for his son. Wayne was an egotistical, condescending jerk who loved the control his position afforded him. When Walter passed away, Wayne added his name to the title—a move that would have infuriated his father. Terry avoided Wayne at all costs, which wasn't hard to do since he was rarely at work. He was either at the gym or on the golf course. The only time he saw him was when he called him to his office to reprimand him about something.

His office was immaculately maintained, uncluttered by anything but office essentials—a computer, an in/out file (with the "in" box perpetually empty), a pen holder that contained only one expensive-looking pen, a telephone placed slightly at an angle, a purple velvet-framed picture of his perfect family, an empty wastebasket, and a paper shredder. Wayne didn't trust anyone, so he shredded everything.

"You left work today and didn't tell anyone," said Wayne, as he squeezed a set of hand-grippers he kept in his desk drawer.

Terry lingered just inside the door of the office. He hoped Wayne wouldn't ask him to sit down. "I'm sorry about that. There was an incident at Miranda's school."

Wayne sat up in his chair. "Not a shooting...?"

"No," replied Terry quickly. "She fell off the monkey bars. Broke her arm." Broke sounded better than sprained, so he went with it. "I had to take her to the hospital."

"Couldn't... ahhh..."

"Hannah?" Terry offered. Boydston never could remember her name. It wasn't his fault, though. He'd never met her. Hannah never came to the office, or, God forbid, an office party.

"Yeah. Hannah. Couldn't she do it?"

"She's having a hard time lately, so I had to go."

Wayne sat back in his chair and folded his arms over his taut midsection, then pointed his head toward the chair in front of his desk, a sign Terry took as a command to come in and sit down.

"She still got that? How long's it been now?"

Terry wanted to tell him it was none of his damn business and to go screw himself, but this was, after all, the man who signed his checks. So he sat down like an obedient dog.

"Just a couple of years. Seven or so," said Terry, fidgeting in the chair. He usually controlled his anxiety by shaking his leg, but the last time he'd been called to Wayne's office, Wayne had pointed it out. He called it "restless leg syndrome," and suggested he get it checked out. Terry didn't want him to know that he'd ignored his advice.

"Is she getting any better?" asked Wayne with a tone of annoyance, rather than sympathy.

"No. Worse. She won't even leave the house now."

"You know," said Wayne, the way a father would parcel out an unsolicited life lesson on to a disinterested son, "Catherine had a case of the blues after we had Carly. It lasted a few weeks but she got over it. Has she seen a doctor?"

"She doesn't trust them. At least not the mental health kind. Thinks they're all quacks."

"Is she at least taking something for it?"

"Just cigarettes," replied Terry, trying to make a joke.

"You let her smoke around your kid?" Wayne asked judgmentally.

Terry was really getting annoyed now. "There's nothing I can do to stop her. Believe me, I've tried."

Wayne leaned forward on his desk and clasped his hands together, like he was about to say grace.

"I'm worried about you, Terry. I have to be able to count on you, and you've got a lot more on your plate since Rick left."

Left? So, thought Terry, *Is that what they're calling fired nowadays?*

"I need you here more. I already let you leave every day to pick up your kid from school."

"But I don't take a lunch break. And I'm only gone an hour."

"There's other times, too. Times when no one knows where you are. Not even Karen."

"It's meetings. Meetings with potential clients. And some loyal ones, too," Terry lied. He couldn't remember the last time he had a meeting with a client outside of work. "'Gotta keep the clients happy.' That's what your dad always used to say."

Terry secretly relished watching Wayne squirm whenever he brought up his father. "Yeah, well, I want you to leave the meetings to me. You have enough on your plate with the clients you already have."

Terry nodded. "Sure. I'll do that from now on."

Wayne eyed him skeptically, then swiveled his chair around to look out his window at the strip mall parking lot. His was the only office with a window that didn't face a brick wall. "Okay. You can go back to work now."

"Thank you," said Terry. He stood up immediately. He couldn't wait to get out of there.

"And I assume you'll be staying later tonight, to make up for the time," stated Wayne, again without a question mark at the end.

"Of course," said Terry docilely, leaving the door slightly ajar. He knew Wayne liked it that way and hoped he'd score a few points for remembering to do so.

But Wayne never turned back around.

Chapter Fourteen
The Swing Would Stay for Now

"It's still there," said Hannah the next morning, as she stared out the kitchen window at the still-intact swing set.

"I got home late last night," Terry said, as he came into the kitchen and started making Miranda's lunch.

"The backyard is off limits to her until it's gone."

He took a deep breath before he spoke. "Hannah, we need to talk."

"You're not leaving me, Terry," she said quietly. "If you do, I'll kill myself."

"You have to stop saying that," he said under his breath. "Miranda hears you."

He knew Miranda would come into the kitchen at any moment. Terry didn't want her to witness yet one more argument first thing in the morning.

Hannah turned to him with tears in her eyes. "Please don't leave me," she said. "I need you."

He placed the knife he'd been using in the sink and turned to her. He could smell the fear on her breath. "I wish there was something I could do."

Hannah picked up the knife and softly traced her fingers over its serrated edge.

"Not leaving me is something you can do," she said.

"I never said I was leaving you," Terry said, as he reached out to her.

"Stop," she said and began to back toward the stove.

He dropped his head and shook it slowly from side to side.

"I'm out of ideas, Hannah. I'm sorry there's nothing I can do for you."

"Do you think I like being like this? Every night, I pray that I'll wake up in the morning and the pain will be gone. But every day it gets worse."

"You're inside the house too much. It'd drive anyone crazy. Maybe if you got out more."

"I can't. It hurts too much. The sun is too bright. The air is too harsh. Everything hurts." And then she added under her breath, "And I'm not crazy."

"I think you need to see a doctor. You were fine before Miranda was born. You can be fine again. They have medications for people like you." He knew it was a mistake the instant he said, "people like you."

"People like me? What's that supposed to mean?"

He didn't respond. There was no point. There was no winning with her.

"And tell me—what's a doctor going to do? Give me a bunch of pills? Then what'll I be, a zombie? Like my father was? Don't you see? People like me don't get better. My father never did."

"But it may be a chemical imbalance. The drugs they have nowadays are different from what your father took."

"Bullshit. Same drugs, different names," she said, as she pulled out a pack of cigarettes from the pocket of her frayed pink robe. Terry remembered the day he gave her that robe. It was the day Miranda was born. She'd worn it nearly every day since.

"Maybe if you cut down on the cigarettes..." he suggested.

"My cigarettes? Are you kidding me? These things save me from going out of my mind," she said, using one to punctuate her point. "If I didn't smoke, I don't know what

I'd do. It's the only thing I have that calms me. Don't ever ask me to stop. Ever!"

Just then, Miranda entered the room, dragging her backpack with the arm that wasn't in the sling.

"Let me get that for you, honey," said Terry, as he took her backpack and inserted her lunch pail inside. "Ready to go?"

"Yup."

"How's your arm?" asked Hannah, as she took a long drag from her cigarette and blew it up toward the yellowed ceiling.

"Okay."

"Do you want to stay home from school?"

"No," said Miranda, quickly. "I'm fine. Ready to go, Daddy?"

"You bet," he said.

Hannah watched them leave the kitchen. They never kissed her goodbye anymore.

***

That evening, Terry asked Miranda. "Honey, would it be okay with you if Daddy took down your swing set?"

"I guess so. If it'll make Mommy feel better," she replied, as if she'd anticipated what he was going to ask.

"But will you miss it?" he pressed. He didn't want Miranda agreeing to something just to appease Hannah.

"No. Not really," she said.

"Not really? So you kind of want it to stay?"

Miranda thought for a moment. "No. I want you to take it down. I'm too old for it, anyway."

***

Terry remembered the weekend day he set aside to put together Miranda's swing set. He had planned to get up early and quickly assemble it. Then he would relax on a lawn chair, he thought, beer in hand, and watch her enjoy the toils of his labor. But things didn't quite work out that way.

It began smoothly enough. He read all the directions cover to cover, resisting the urge to assemble it out of sequence. He had a nice level area of the yard in which to build it and all the tools the manual suggested at his disposal. But as diligently as he followed the instructions, when he was finished, there were multiple parts missing and various (structurally important-looking) parts left over. He was convinced that the manufacturer screwed up. In the end, he had to hire a local handyman to review his work and apply the finishing touches that he knew were out of his scope of capability (like anchoring it down with cement). His pride mattered little when it came to Miranda's safety.

Like most kids, it took Miranda a while to get the hang of swinging.

"You have to pump your legs, honey," he urged her repeatedly. For weeks she tried but couldn't seem to master the task without him assisting her. He didn't mind, though. He loved the fact that she needed him.

Then, one day, she got the hang of it. Terry stood back with a sense of pride but also a feeling of sadness in his heart. Her accomplishment symbolized one more step closer to independence. He dreaded the day when she no longer needed him.

**

That night, by the light emanating from the back porch, Terry began the arduous task of dismantling the swing set. But he didn't get far. Over time and seasons, moisture had rusted the nuts and bolts, and as hard as he tried, he couldn't get them to budge.

The swing would stay for now.

Chapter Fifteen
You're a Sex Addict

Lois Patrick had seen them come and go for years. None of them stayed. She knew her daughter's propensity towards promiscuity had begun at a young age, and she knew the reason why. And it wasn't her inherent Irish libido.

Before it all began, they'd been as close as any mother and daughter could be. But once she found out, she could barely look at Renee anymore. She knew it wasn't her fault, but she still couldn't forgive her. Their once-tight bond had been irrevocably broken and they became merely co-workers.

Recently, she wanted something more again. She was tired of the fighting, the resentment, and the guilt. She wanted her daughter back. She didn't know if Renee felt the same way, though, and she was too afraid to make the first move; to be the first one to reach out. What if she was rejected? That would make Lois feel worse than if she hadn't tried. It was better to wonder than to get that response. And what if Renee stopped talking to her? Even though they fought constantly, at least they communicated.

How could they run the store if they weren't on speaking terms? Where would she live? Lois had moved in with Renee six years ago, after her third hip surgery, and Renee tended to her. She was a good daughter in many ways, and not so good in others.

They shared a double-wide on twenty acres. That much property would cost a fortune down south, but not in Porterville. The trailer was small, but they didn't need much space. The upkeep on twenty acres, plus running the hardware store, kept them too busy to maintain a bigger place. They both had their own rooms, and pretty much stayed out of each other's way.

Lois never stopped thinking about it. Never stopped hoping things would go back to the way they were. There was so much they needed to talk about. So many years of hiding from the truth. Where would they begin? Was it too much to consider? Was it too late?

Her thoughts were interrupted by the sound of the bell chiming over the door. At first, she loved that bell. Every time she heard it, she knew someone with money was walking through that door and she was going to do her best to make sure they spent some of it before they left. In the beginning, business was brisk. They paid off the place after only seven years.

Over the years, though, she began to hate the sound of that bell. Whereas once it represented hope, now it only gave her a headache. Was it someone wanting to return something without a receipt? Or a talkative tightwad who'd take up all her time and then leave without buying anything? Or someone who'd complain they could get things for a lot less at Home Depot? All of those types annoyed the hell out of her.

But none of them annoyed her as much as one of Renee's sleazy suitors sauntering in with sexual desperation written all over his face.

She craned her neck toward the entrance to see who it was this time.

It was him again. The new one.

"Back for more, I see," she said with a weary smile.

She got down off the footstool she was using to stock shelves and placed her hands on her hips, feeling the desire to be a bit more combative with this one than she ever was with the others. She didn't know why, but she sensed he was different from the rest.

"Yes," he answered. He looked confused. "Is that okay?"

"I'd be careful if I were you. You're playing with fire with that one. Once she sets her mind on something, or someone, she doesn't let go."

"I don't know what you're talking about," he said.

"Don't play dumb with me. I know why you're here. I'm just trying to warn you. Don't ask me why. Maybe 'cause I sense that you're better than the rest."

"Better?"

"Yes, better," she reiterated. "Better than them. Better than her."

"I'm not here for what you think."

She was not letting up. "Oh, yeah? What *are* you here for?"

"Look. I don't want to have this discussion with you. I just want to know if she's here."

She stared at him for a moment, and then shook her head and went back to stocking shelves. "In her office. Doing book work." Then she added, "Enter at your own risk."

***

"It's behind the front counter," said Renee, disengaged, not bothering to look up from her pile of paperwork. She knew it was Terry because she'd heard every word of his conversation with her mother. "The old lady out there will get it for you if you ask kindly."

"I'll get it when I leave. Thanks."

She raised her head and looked at him. He looked better than he did the first couple of times. And he smelled different. "So what do you want?" she asked.

"I came back to get the picture."

"Like I said, it's…"

"And," he interrupted her, "To tell you something."

She sat back in her chair. "And what's that?"

"I wanted to tell you that you were right. Home Depot sucks."

Renee smiled in spite of herself. "You wearing cologne?"

"Yeah," he admitted, looking sheepish. "I usually don't wear it. Probably put too much on. Do you like it?"

"No," she said bluntly. "I like your natural smell."

He smiled. "I'll never wear it again. Promise."

She got up and walked toward the open door, keeping her eyes on him the entire time.

"You know what I think?" she asked, as she closed the door and locked it. "I think you came back here because you like me. I'm more fun than that old ball and chain you got at home. And, to tell you the truth, I don't mind that. I don't mind being the fun one. I will never get married if I have to end up being the alternative to fun."

She moved away from the door and walked over to him. She was standing inches from him, but not touching his body. Her breasts, barely constrained by the snaps of her red Western shirt, rose and fell with each breath she took.

She could tell he was struggling to retain his composure.

She reached out and took his hands. "That cologne you're wearing? It's starting to grow on me." She cupped his groin. "Anything growing on you?"

He jumped back as if he'd been shocked by an electric fence. "*Stop!*" And then he added, "Please."

She let out a sigh of impatience and folded her arms in exasperation. "Are we going to do this again? I'm really too old for these games."

He took a timid step toward her. "I'm not playing games. I like talking to you. You're fun, and funny, and different. But that's enough for me. For now."

"For now?" she asked. "They always keep it open."

He began to play with his wedding ring, saying nothing, his head down.

She gave him a long, penetrating look, and then took a pen from behind her ear and wrote something on a Post-it. She ripped it from the pad and handed it to him. "My number. For when you're ready. Until then, don't waste my time."

"I can't. I shouldn't," he said, staring at the Post-it.

"Take it, for Chrissake. It's only a number. You may get stranded somewhere and need someone to call. It's not like your wife can come and get you."

He nodded and quickly took the number, stashing it in his pocket.

"I wouldn't put it there. She'll find it and call. I don't want to have to deal with her."

"She won't find it. I do the laundry."

Renee wasn't surprised by his admission. He seemed like the kind of guy who'd do laundry.

"Of course you do," she said, and then she returned to her chair behind her desk and resumed her bookwork.

"You can go now. And don't step foot in my hardware store again until you're ready."

"Ready?" he asked.

She looked at him over the edge of her glasses. "You know what I mean."

He knew exactly what she meant.

***

Renee listened as Terry asked Lois for Miranda's picture.

Moments after that, she heard the bell ring as he left the store.

She took off her glasses and rubbed her eyes. She was tired —in so many ways. She felt like crying but wouldn't allow herself to; not over a man. No man was worth her tears, not even Terry.

She heard Lois shuffle down the hall toward the office. She looked up and saw her standing in the doorway with a disagreeable look on her face.

"Don't look at me that way," Renee said.

"I wish I didn't have to," Lois said, with that attitude in her voice that always got to Renee. It dripped of disappointment and pity and Renee couldn't stand it anymore. Who was she to judge her? She was just as guilty as Renee; even more so. And yet, for years, she'd made Renee feel "less than."

As if she needed her own mother to make her feel what she already felt about herself.

Lois sniffed, and then walked away shaking her head.

Renee felt a wave of anger wash over her entire body. She sprang from her chair and stormed down the hall after Lois, adrenaline pulsating through her veins.

"Well, you don't have to, Mother!"

Lois turned around and said, calmly, "Oh, Renee. When are you going to learn? They only want you for sex."

"Not him. He didn't even want sex. He just wanted to be my friend. He liked me enough to walk away because he knew it would lead to something. And it probably would have."

"Guess he was one of the smarter ones," said Lois coldly.

"You're right. He is smarter than the rest. And nicer. And sweeter. But he's miserable. Sometimes divorce isn't such a bad thing." And then Renee decided to go there. "Maybe if you'd have left Dad, things would have been different."

Lois shuddered visibly. She clearly wasn't prepared for this conversation.

"Don't you think I considered divorce?" Lois said, her face flaming red.

"Then why didn't you? What stopped you?"

"I don't know. I honestly don't know . . ."

"Yes, you do. You have to. No mother would allow what you allowed. *Tell me!*"

Lois looked at her, as tears welled up in her eyes. "What difference would it have made if I left? The damage was already done."

"Damage?"

The word sent a cold chill down Renee's spine. So that's how her mother thought of her—as *damaged*. Damaged beyond repair. Too damaged to save. Too damaged to love.

She knew she had to get out of there—away from the store, away from her mother, away from the pain.

"Wait!" Lois screamed after her.

But Renee couldn't wait. Couldn't stop. Couldn't turn back.

Within moments, Stud-Muffin was carrying her away at breakneck speed. She had no idea where she was going, but she wasn't turning back.

***

Lois was alone now, surrounded by the hardware store's numerous tools, all designed to fix, to mend, to restore. But nothing on those shelves could repair a broken heart.

She stood motionless, staring without seeing, unable to feel anything.

Until she did.

It was a pain in her chest so sharp and so fierce that it brought her to her knees. The pain was relentless. It felt like someone was squeezing her heart with a vise-grip. She prayed she'd hear that annoying bell over the door ring one more time. But the only sound she heard was the whir of the oscillating ceiling fan.

And her last breath leaving her body, signaling her exit from this life.

***

Renee walked into the seedy, dark bar and smelled stale beer in the air. Instantly, she felt comforted. The musty smell and the country music—it was like visiting an old friend who didn't judge or challenge you, but only welcomed you with open arms.

The place was empty except for the bartender, Danny. He was familiar. He was comfortable. He was always ready.

She sat at the bar and nodded, and he knew what that meant. She wanted a shot and she wanted it now. He obliged her, and then refilled it the second she slammed it back down on the bar.

"When do you get off?" she asked, trying to avoid her reflection in the mirror behind the bar.

He leaned in toward her. "You're the only one here. Can close for an hour, if you want."

"Won't take an hour," she said, as she tossed back the second shot. She slid the glass down the bar until it crashed into a bowl of stale peanuts. "Lock the doors."

"You got it." He leapt over the bar, locked the door, and then flipped the "Open" sign to "Closed."

She began to unbutton her jeans as he closed in on her and hoisted her up onto the bar.

He was in her within seconds. As she rolled back her head, she caught her upside down reflection in the mirror. Her face looked like an image from a demonic film. And it horrified her.

She shoved Danny off of her and quickly pulled up her jeans.

"I can't do this. I've got to get out of here."

"What's the matter? Did I do something wrong?"

"No. It's me. I just… can't."

Danny kicked a barstool over. "Goddammit! You went and got me all hot and bothered! What am I supposed to do now?"

"I don't know and I don't care. This was a mistake."

Danny shuffled over to her, his pants down around his ankles like a shackled prisoner. "Are you sure? I'll be more gentle next time."

"There's not going to be a next time, Danny," Renee said, as she handed him a ten dollar bill. "Here. This should cover my shots."

Danny pulled up his pants. "Keep it. I guess I owe you for the little we done," he sulked.

Renee crinkled up the bill in her fist and threw it at him. "Take the money. I'm not a prostitute."

"No, Renee, you ain't a prostitute," he said as he tightened his belt. "You're a sex addict."

Part Two

Chapter Sixteen
It Took Too Much Energy to Fight

Watching TV took Hannah's mind off her own problems. She watched it all day long and fell asleep every night with it still on. She hated to turn it off. She hated the silence, the dull hum of emptiness. It was like all her friends had left the party and she was alone, relegated to picking up the remnants of the evening, each dirty plate and soiled napkin triggering a memory of the night's events.

In college, she discovered the soaps. She and her girlfriends would schedule their classes around their favorite daytime programs. They'd cling to every word as they munched on buttered popcorn and drank diet soda by the gallon. Those times represented some of her best memories.

But once she had Miranda, she couldn't take the soaps anymore. The actors were too pretty and their lives, although ripe with strife, were played out against the backdrop of their richly decorated homes and unrealistic professions. And eventually, no matter how horrible the storyline, everything got resolved. She knew life wasn't that way.

That was why she switched over to the twenty-four-hour news stations. Life was bad and they weren't afraid to report it. Fox was her favorite. She knew each anchor by name. She knew which ones were married, single, or newly divorced. She knew how many kids they had and where they spent their holidays. And she ate up every word they said. She never doubted their veracity, and she heeded their warnings and advice. She trusted every word that came out of their mouths. They were her friends.

***

Terry couldn't stand the incessant sound of the TV at all hours, and especially the depressing news station Hannah was addicted to.

As a result, he avoided the bedroom until she had fallen asleep, which usually wasn't until after midnight. Once he was sure she was asleep, he'd creep in and quietly switch off the TV. She never woke up. Once she was out, she was out.

Unless, of course, there was an earthquake.

Every night, before he went to bed, he took a very long shower. It was the only time he could really be alone with no one bothering him. It was just him and his thoughts; thoughts that would circle around in his head like the soap sliding down his body and rotating around the drain.

After his shower, he'd stand naked in front of the mirror and observe his ever-changing body. Lately, it was all going downhill. His once taut midsection had lost definition and was beginning to jut outwards. It wasn't as noticeable when he was examining it straight on, but when he turned to the side he looked like one of those middle-aged men he'd stare at from his car as they sauntered across the intersection with protruding pouches, looking like Alfred Hitchcock making a cameo in one of his films.

And then there was the increasing body hair. Stubborn, errant gray strands had begun sprouting up like weeds on his back, shoulders, and even in his ears. He plucked them as soon as he spotted them, but he knew he was fighting a losing battle. He wasn't getting any younger and he just had to accept it.

It was just like everything else in his life. Acceptance was the only way he knew how to cope.

It took too much energy to fight.

Chapter Seventeen
And He Knew It Was Time to Pay Him Another Visit

Terry wasn't "ready." At least not in the way that Renee meant it, and he didn't know if he'd ever be. So, it was several weeks before he returned, but he didn't go inside. Nor did he let her know he was back. Rather, he parked his car just far enough down the road to see, but not be seen. Just far enough to make out the entrance to the hardware store. He was hoping to get a glimpse of her, but afraid she might see him, and then, who knew what?

Why couldn't he let her go? Even he didn't know the answer to that question. Why was he so attracted to her? Yes, she was attractive, but his feelings for her didn't have anything to do with her looks.

It was the way she made him feel. She made him feel like more of a man than he'd ever felt in his life. Her sense of humor was alien to him—it was so shocking and sexual, but it had grown on him. Her bluntness was refreshing because it left nothing unsaid. And her attraction to him made him feel desirable again. Young again.

And then it dawned on him. He knew why he went back.

She made him feel alive again.

He sat in his car, contemplating what to do. If he returned, he'd better be "ready." Renee made that very clear to him.

He put the car in drive and began inching toward the parking lot. As the store gradually came into view, he began to shake uncontrollably. Memories began to rush back into his consciousness. Memories almost too painful to endure. When would they subside? His heart was racing so fast he felt as if it would burst out of his chest like an alien in a gory horror film. His skin crawled. He wanted to escape from his own body and run as fast as he could away from the pain and anxiety.

He knew what was happening. It had happened on the first day he met Renee.

And he knew it was time to pay him another visit.

Chapter Eighteen
I'm Here to Help

Terry didn't like to talk to anyone about his problems. He learned early that it's best to keep things inside. The more you reveal, the more vulnerable you become. And then people take advantage of your weaknesses. That's what his parents did after their bitter divorce, and it emotionally destroyed him.

Even during the good times with Hannah, he never really let her "in." He always kept a cool distance when it came to his feelings.

But a few weeks before he met Renee, he knew he couldn't keep it in any longer.

He began seeing a therapist.

The therapist asked all his clients to call him Marv, so he complied, even though it made him uncomfortable to refer to a total stranger by a nickname. He wasn't a psychiatrist, just a plain old therapist. Terry had decided to start small and, if he had to, move up to the real deal.

He had been seeing Marv three times a week for several months, and he liked him right from the beginning. He was a good listener and didn't ask too many stupid questions. His office was warm and homey. He kept the lights low and rarely spoke above a whisper. Marv had a grandfatherly quality about him (perhaps it was the knitted sweaters and gray beard) that attracted Terry, since he'd never known his own grandfather. Marv always offered Terry coffee before their sessions began and Terry always said no because the smell of coffee reminded him of Hannah's breath in the morning.

He sat rigidly on a soft leather sofa, his feet planted firmly on the ground. He couldn't imagine lying down and talking to the ceiling like they did in the movies. He answered most questions briefly and vaguely. It was all he could manage. He couldn't be completely open with Marv. Not yet, at least. He spent most of his forty-five-minute sessions talking about Renee and the way she made him feel. He never talked about Hannah and Miranda.

"How long has it been since you've seen her?" asked Marv, before taking a sip of his coffee.

"I don't know," Terry lied. He knew the exact day he walked out of the hardware store after telling her he couldn't go on with their relationship. *Relationship.* That seemed like the wrong word. But, it certainly wasn't a friendship. No friend ever made Terry feel the way Renee did. "Maybe a month."

"Do you miss her?"

Okay, Terry thought, *First stupid question.* Didn't he know the answer already? How many hours had they talked only about Renee? "Sometimes. But then I stop myself. I can't go there."

"What's the worst thing that could happen?"

"I would be tempted to… I don't want to be unfaithful."

"Unfaithful? But—"

"I can't…"

Terry was about to continue, when something caught his eye. It was a painting Marv had hanging behind his desk. Terry got up and walked toward it so he could observe it up close. It was one of those mass-produced reproductions depicting cozy scenes of storybook houses, designed to give the spectator a sense of peace and serenity.

Terry stared at the painting, mesmerized by every detail. The cottage had a cobblestone exterior and one lone dormer jutting out of its gray-shingled roof. It was surrounded by a low, crooked fence and sporadic foliage. A tall tree, most likely an oak, grew out of the frame of the picture. The home had an arched doorway, undoubtedly unlocked due to the cottage's isolated and remote setting. Every French window was lit from the inside of the house, while smoke billowed out of the chimney. It was so bright inside the house it appeared that the entire interior was engulfed in flames.

He walked unsteadily back to the sofa and sat down, his face ashen.

"Terry?" asked Marv, concerned. "Are you all right?"

Terry couldn't speak. He felt like he was going to faint, and so he did something that surprised even him—he reclined on the sofa and stared up at the ceiling. He began to take deep breaths, and felt the dizziness abating.

He heard Marv say something, but it sounded like it was coming from a distant tunnel.

"Would you like to end our session?"

Terry covered his eyes with the inside crook of his elbow.

"No, but if you don't mind, I'd like to lie here for a while and not say anything. If that's all right with you."

He heard Marv shift in his chair. And then he said, "Of course it's all right. This is your time."

For a moment there was silence, except for Terry's breathing, which sounded like a death rattle.

"Terry?" asked Marv. "Are you all right? What happened?"

But Terry didn't answer.

"Take all the time you need," said Marv, soothingly. "I'm here to help."

Chapter Nineteen
Not At a Time Like This

It seemed like almost every day Terry received a call from someone sounding worried and concerned and wanting to come in and talk about their insurance. They were confused about all the new changes. He could tell which clients were Republicans and which were Democrats by how they referred to it: Republicans called it Obamacare and Democrats called it the Affordable Care Act. What they all had in common was that they wanted to save money, to find out if there was any way to cut back.

At first he took it in stride, telling himself that everyone suffered during hard economic times. But it seemed the insurance business was getting pounded the hardest, and it started to wear on him. His job used to be a no-brainer; something he could practically do in his sleep. He never worried about making his quota. He never thought he could lose his job.

But then again, neither did Albert Davis, the bedraggled man sitting across the desk from him. When Albert sat down, the first thing Terry noticed about him was his fingernails. They were clean. He'd known Albert for almost five years, and in all that time he'd never seen him without dirt under his nails from working on car engines all day. But ever since a year ago, when Albert was laid off from the auto repair shop he'd worked at since he was a teenager, he no longer had a job that required him to get his hands dirty. Filling out job applications and standing in the unemployment line didn't get you dirty. It just made you feel that way.

Albert had just turned fifty and he confessed to Terry, with tears welling up in his eyes, that he felt like his life was over. His wife was supporting the family and her job didn't offer health insurance, he told Terry. That meant Albert had to pay out-of-pocket to protect himself and his family, just in case something tragic happened. And now that he'd turned fifty, his rates had shot up and he didn't know how he was going to keep up with the increase. Writing those huge checks every month was getting harder and harder. So, like the throngs of people who'd been in Terry's office before him, Albert was looking for a few "savings"—just until he got back on his feet.

"Are you sure you want to cancel your comp and collision?" asked Terry. He was concerned. He knew too many people who canceled their comp and collision just before they got into an accident. That was the way life worked. At least that's how he saw life. Fate was never kind.

"I have to cut back somewhere," said Albert. "Not like I do much driving anyway, since I lost my job."

"Things will turn around," said Terry, trying to sound as positive as possible.

"Yeah. That's what I keep hearing."

"It will," said Terry, as he made the adjustments to the policy. "I'll make the change. As long as you're comfortable with your coverage, that's all that matters."

"Of course I'm not comfortable with it, but it'll have to do for now."

Terry looked up at Albert and noticed Kevin peeking in the door. He was sweating profusely and his face was ashen.

"You're with a client," said Kevin, pointing out the obvious. "I'll come back later."

Albert cocked his head around and saw Kevin pacing just outside the door, looking like he was about to come unglued.

"No," said Albert, getting up. "That's okay. I'd better get out of here before I'm guilted into something else I can't afford."

"I'm not guilting you," said Terry. "I'm looking out for you. And your family."

"Yeah," said Albert with a faraway look in his eyes. "Me, too. I'll come back another day. It's not like I have a job to go to."

And then he ambled out of the office like a wounded, abandoned puppy looking for someone to either rescue him or put him to sleep.

As soon as he was gone, Kevin blurted out, "I've been let go." He added, *"Fired!"* with emphasis.

Terry sat up in his chair. "What? Why?"

"Downsizing. Least that's what he told me."

For a moment, Terry was speechless. For all of Kevin's quirks, he was a solid insurance salesman with a bevy of loyal clients.

"What are you going to do?" asked Terry, wondering how long it'd be until he asked himself the same question.

"Dunno. He just told me."

"Sit down. Please. You need to take a second and relax."

"Okay," he said. He sat, and then immediately got up again.

"No, I'm too jumpy right now. I knew it was coming when Boydston gave you the bulk of Rick's workload. I've been preparing. Socking a little away every month. Sending out my resume. I'll be fine. The Lord will provide."

"Do you want me to talk with Wayne? Maybe I can get him to change his mind."

"And have him fire you instead? Keep doing what you're doing and hope you're not next. It was Rick first. Now me. I'd keep my head down if I were you. You know, there's nothing stopping him from hiring a couple of green college kids who'd work for a lot less than we make." After a beat, he corrected himself. "Made."

Terry's head was spinning. What if he were next? What would happen then?

"Sit down. You have to calm down."

Kevin finally sat down, took off his tie, and tossed it in the overflowing trashcan next to Terry's desk.

"I always hated wearing a tie. Next job I get, I ain't wearing no tie. They're stupid. They don't have any use. They're not like a belt. A belt at least has a purpose; it holds up your pants. But what's the purpose of a tie? They're only for looks and it makes no sense. Who invented them, anyway?"

Terry listened to Kevin ramble. He knew Kevin needed to vent, let off steam, and talk about anything other than what just happened to him.

"I'm so sorry, Kevin. Can I help with anything? Do you want some help clearing out your office?" Terry offered.

"No, thanks anyway," said Kevin. "Nothing to clear out. Just things. They're not important. Jesus died wearing nothing but a piece of cloth."

Kevin dropped his head down, clasped his hands, and began to pray.

Terry stared at the bald spot on the top of his head, giving him a moment.

After a few minutes, Kevin looked up at Terry. "There's something I've always wanted to ask you, Terry."

"What?" asked Terry, knowing the subject before Kevin even asked the question. Was he saved? Did he know the Lord? Was Christ in his heart?

"Do you think I'd make a good minister?" asked Kevin.

"Sure," answered Terry, hoping Kevin wouldn't detect the disingenuousness in his reply. Terry didn't think he'd make a very good preacher at all. He wasn't a churchgoer, but the ones he'd seen on TV were full of confidence and swagger and blustery talk. Kevin was too meek, too self-conscious to inspire anyone, much less a congregation of wide-eyed worshipers.

But he'd never tell Kevin that. Not at a time like this.

Chapter Twenty
Preparation Saves Lives

Hannah lit a cigarette as soon as Terry broke the news to her about Kevin. *"Jesus Christ!* What if you're next?"

"Would you keep your voice down?" said Terry. "Miranda will wake up and hear you."

"What will we do if you lose your job?"

"I don't know. I'll find another."

"In this economy? Good luck."

Terry hesitated before dropping the next bombshell. "Wayne says I'll be working longer hours." And then he added: "You may have to pick up Miranda from school from now on."

"Oh, no. I won't," Hannah said, as she shoved her hands into a pair of blue, heavy-duty rubber gloves. "You'll just have to work something out." She began to scrub vigorously on the dishes. "You're doing this on purpose, aren't you?!" Terry released an audible sound of disgust. "You're devising this plan to get me out of the house." She turned to him and eyed him disbelievingly. "Did Kevin really even get fired?"

Terry stared at her for a moment, then shook his head incredulously and left the room.

"You probably don't even have to work longer hours!" she shouted after him. "You're probably seeing someone on the side!"

***

Hannah reached for her cigarette and inhaled deeply, still wearing her thick rubber gloves. After a few more drags, she stubbed it out in the crudely molded ceramic ashtray Miranda made for her last Christmas. The ashtray was overflowing with butts. The butts used to have lipstick stains on them, but she'd given up on wearing makeup years ago.

***

Terry placed the vase of fresh poppies on Miranda's nightstand and was tiptoeing back toward the bedroom door when he heard her voice fill the darkness.

"Daddy?"

He'd tried so hard to be quiet and it startled him. "Yes, Sweetie?"

"Are you seeing another mommy?"

His shoulders slumped. So she'd heard the whole fight with Hannah. He hated knowing that it had kept her awake when she should have been sound asleep, dreaming about the sweet, innocent things that girls her age had a right to dream about.

"No, of course not," he assured her in the darkness. "I'd never do that to Mommy, and I'd never do that to you. Now try to get some sleep."

Miranda let out a sigh of relief so long and loud it was though she'd been holding her breath for hours.

***

The following morning Terry was in the bathroom, shaving, when he heard Hannah scream out.

"Oh, my God! Terry, get in here. Quick!"

He rushed into the bedroom holding his razor, his face half shaved.

"What is it?"

She was staring at the TV, a cigarette dangling from her lips.

He came around the side of the TV and stood next to her. It was one of Fox's several breaking news stories that appeared after every commercial. All he could see were burning houses and fire trucks and a bleached blonde reporter breathlessly outlining events that were unfolding in real time.

"This house in Maryland had a gas leak," said Hannah, her voice shaking. "Blew up in the middle of the night killing everyone inside. Every house on the street caught fire. A whole block wiped out in one night. Can you believe it?"

Terry stared at the TV, trying to sympathize. But Maryland was on the other side of the country and terrible things were happening all over the place. The next breaking news story would be just as bad, if not worse. He had to pick and choose what to be upset about. He wasn't like Hannah. Everything upset her. Everything was bad news.

Maybe if he didn't have so many problems of his own, he'd care. But until things changed in his life, he'd never have the energy or capability to take on the woes of the world. He went back into the bathroom and resumed shaving. Through the closed door, he could hear her still going on about it.

When he came out of the bathroom, she was sitting on the edge of the bed, still mesmerized by the story. As he began to get dressed, she said, "You need to check the batteries in the smoke detectors. Don't remember the last time you did that. They're probably all dead."

"I doubt a smoke detector would have saved anyone from a gas explosion."

"Better to be safe than sorry. And call the gas company. I want them to make sure we don't have a leak. I've been smelling a weird odor lately. Nothing wrong with being prepared. Preparation saves lives."

Chapter Twenty-One
And He Didn't Look Happy

Marv persistently, but gently, encouraged Terry to return to the hardware store to address his feelings for Renee and bring closure to something that was obviously bothering him and interfering with his ability to move on. Terry didn't like the word *closure*. It sounded like a silly psychobabble term, so he resisted.

But Marv was right about one thing—he couldn't get Renee out of his mind, and it was affecting his ability to function. The more he tried, the more she monopolized his every thought—both sleeping and waking. He knew he had to do something about it. So, one day, he decided to go back. He wasn't *ready* in the way Renee meant it, and he didn't know how that would go over with her. All he knew is that he had to see her again. Where that would lead, he didn't have a clue.

He sat in his car, a safe distance away from the store, but near enough to have an unobstructed view of the pebble parking lot, contemplating his decision to return. He knew he had to do it, get *closure*, but he felt anxious and frightened nonetheless. He took a deep breath, shrugged off his feelings of apprehension, pressed the gas pedal slightly, and crept toward the store. He was going so slowly his speed barely registered on the speedometer.

Honk!!

The man in the car behind Terry laid on his horn. He bolted upright in his seat as the car maneuvered around him. Terry could see the man give him the finger as he sped away. Normally this gesture would have bothered Terry, but not today. He had more important things on his mind.

As Terry got closer to the entrance of the parking lot, he noticed that the sign over the front door—the sign that had caught his attention and drew him into the store in the first place—was dark.

He had to think about what day it was. Tuesday. There was no reason for her to close the store on a Tuesday. Or perhaps it wasn't closed. Maybe she just forgot to turn the sign on. Everyone forgets the little things sometimes—although Renee didn't seem like the kind of person to forget the little things.

He flipped on his turn signal. He didn't know why. No one used turn signals in this town, especially this far out. But it was a force of habit and Terry was a habitual person.

He stepped lightly on the gas again and eased into the driveway. He knew that if she was working, she'd surely hear his tires traveling over the pebbles at this point. There was no turning back now; she'd have to know that she had a customer. She'd probably wait until the bell over the door rang before checking to see who it was.

He parked his car, but left the car doors unlocked. He got out of his car and shut his door ever so quietly. Then he began to walk toward the store. When he got close to the door, he saw the sign in the window. It read, "Closed."

Closed? he wondered. *Why would she close the store on a weekday?*

She couldn't afford to close during business hours if she was competing with the big chain stores. Something was definitely wrong.

He tried the door, but it was locked. He went to the window, wiped away the dusty film coating it, and peered in. No lights, no activity. Even the oscillating ceiling fan was motionless.

Did she go on vacation? Out of the question. Renee wasn't the type to take a vacation. Was she ill? If she was, surely her mother would be there to keep the doors open. Things didn't add up. Now his curiosity was really piqued. He had to find out what the hell was going on.

And the person who could tell him had just turned into the parking lot.

And he didn't look happy.

Chapter Twenty-Two
Wives Go Through Phone Bills

"Who the hell are you?" barked the rotund middle-aged man, as he struggled to hoist his hefty body out of the cab of his mammoth truck.

"I'm a customer," Terry said. "Sort of a regular, I guess you could say."

"Never seen you before," he said as he spit a gob of thick, black liquid on the ground.

Terry made a mental note to watch where he stepped when he returned to his car.

"I haven't been around lately, but I used to stop by occasionally. Usually around this time."

The man approached Terry and looked him up and down. "You don't look like you're from around here. What's your name?" he asked suspiciously.

"Terry Boyle," said Terry, stiffly, without offering his hand.

"Name's Otis," he said. "So, what are you doing here?"

"I… need to buy some smoke detectors."

Otis shrugged his thick shoulders. "Gonna have to go somewhere else. This place is closed."

"Closed? For how long?"

"Don't know. Maybe forever."

"Forever? I don't understand."

"Been closed ever since the funeral."

"Funeral? Who died?" asked Terry, anxiously.

"You ain't heard? Thought you was a regular."

"I am!" he snapped. "I said I haven't been around!"

Otis leaned toward Terry and pointed his pudgy finger in his face. "No need to yell at me."

"I'm sorry," said Terry, exasperated. "I just want to know who died."

"Who'd you say you were, again?" probed Otis further, obviously enjoying watching Terry get all hot and bothered.

Terry fought the urge to grab Otis's fat neck and choke the answer out of him. "My name is Terry Boyle. Could you just tell me who the hell died?"

"Renee's mom," he said, and then he turned his back on Terry and mounted the wooden stairs that led to the entrance door.

"Lois? Oh my God. When?" asked Terry.

"'Bout a month ago."

"How?"

"Heart attack. Came on sudden. Renee found her behind the counter."

Terry felt a desperate desire to find her. Console her. Hold her. "Where is she?"

Otis turned and looked at him. "Why do you want to know?"

"I just do," said Terry.

Otis turned his back again and began to unlock the door. "She's keeping to herself. Doesn't want to see anyone right now. 'Cept a few of us. She asked me to check out the place once a day. Make sure there ain't anyone suspicious lurking around. And if you don't mind my saying, you seem mighty suspicious."

"Look," said Terry, trying to keep his anger in check. "Renee and I are friends."

"Then why don't you call her?" said Otis, as he removed the key from the door and shoved it into his back pocket. "You got her number?"

Terry paused for a second. "Yes."

"Then call her. Might not answer, though. Not really in a talkative mood lately." Otis began to close the door in Terry's face. "I'd be careful, though," warned Otis, just before closing it all the way. "Wives go through phone bills."

Chapter Twenty-Three
Trying and Failing was Worse Than Not Trying at All

Terry turned over the kitchen looking for his keys. He was sure he'd put them where he always did—on the counter next to the toaster oven (Hannah refused to use a microwave because they "leaked radiation")—but they weren't there.

Hannah watched as he scrambled around the room like a kid on an Easter egg hunt.

"Why don't we celebrate here? I'll make a cake. Her favorite kind," she said, as she took a drag off of her cigarette.

"It's Miranda's birthday and she wants to go to the Olive Garden. She loves that place. You know that."

Hannah leaned against the counter, her mouth turned into a downward pout. "You'll probably have more fun without me, anyway."

He knew she was trying to make him feel bad for leaving her at home, but he wasn't giving in. Not this time. "That's not true. It'd make her birthday if you came along."

"You know I can't."

"Suit yourself," he said. He wasn't in the mood to placate her tonight. "Have you seen my keys? I swear I put them on the counter when I came home."

Hannah acted as though she didn't hear the question. "I hate this. I hate living this way," she said. "I wish it'd go away."

"I'm going to call a doctor if this goes on much longer," he said, as he continued his search. "Whether you like it or not."

"No, you won't. I can get better on my own," she said. "I've been having some good days lately. Yesterday when you were gone, I sat on the back porch. The sun felt good on my face. Didn't hurt at all."

"That's good," he said. He stopped and looked at her. "In fact, that's great. You should do more of that."

"But today it came back," she said. She was fighting back tears. "It never lasts."

He took a step toward her, prompting her to move to the other side of the butcher-block island. She began to cry, but he didn't console her; not when Miranda was waiting to celebrate her birthday.

He went back to looking for his keys. Then he heard it—a jingling noise. He turned and saw Hannah dangling his car keys between her fingers.

"You had them all along," he fumed. "Why did you do that?"

"I wanted you to stay home. I'm afraid here all by myself."

"You're alone all day long," he said. "Now give them to me."

"But it's nighttime. It's harder at night. And darker."

"We won't be late. It's a school night."

She dropped the keys on the island and slid them over to him. He scooped them up just before they fell off the edge.

"Miranda!" he called out. "Time to go."

***

After they left, Hannah could barely move a muscle. It was devastating for her to know she was missing out on her daughter's eighth birthday. Eight years old and Miranda still seemed like a stranger to her. She knew she was screwing up as a mother, but she felt powerless to do anything about it.

She was so tired. Tired of feeling like a terrible mother. Tired of her crippling emotional illness, which neither Terry nor Miranda understood. She knew she had to do something about her condition or she'd lose everything. Terry was going to leave her and he was going to take Miranda with him, and she'd be left alone. She couldn't bear the thought of that.

***

She stood on the back porch feeling the warm evening air wash over her frail skin, and was comforted by it. The lights at the neighbor's house were on. She could see the people inside moving about, going on with their business. She'd never met them, nor did she want to. She didn't want to be judged by them.

She looked down and noticed the metal air-conditioning unit at the bottom of the stairs. Its factory sticker was peeling at the corners, shriveled up and indecipherable due to exposure to the weather over the years. If she could make it to the bottom step, she'd rip it off. No one read those instructions anyway.

She decided to make that her goal.

Focus, she told herself. *Get to the bottom step and rip off that useless sticker. Baby steps.*

She took one step down and then stopped. That one step was a huge milestone for her. Yesterday she'd made it onto the porch, but then couldn't muster up the courage to go any further.

But this time she was determined to make it all the way down. She took another step.

She halted abruptly when she heard an unsettling noise. It sounded like a bird, but she couldn't be sure. It could be anything. It took all her might not to turn around and run back into the safety of the house.

But she was more fixated than ever about making it to the bottom step. If she could make it that far, perhaps she could continue on. Maybe even make it to Miranda's swing set.

When she was a child, she loved swinging on a swing set. She relished the power she felt as she pumped her legs, propelling her to go higher and higher—so high sometimes that she feared she'd do a complete loop around the top of the set.

She heard it again, that strange, unfamiliar noise. What was it? She was petrified of the unknown. Her body began to shake uncontrollably. She felt weak. What if she fainted? Who would find her? Would the neighbors hear her if she cried out? She realized she couldn't go any further.

She clenched her eyes shut, turned around, and fumbled her way back to the comfort of the house. She never made it to the peeling sticker, much less the swing set. She tried, but failed. Trying and failing was worse than not trying at all.

Chapter Twenty-Four
Life Really Could Change

Miranda watched all the happy families seated around her at the Olive Garden—laughing, talking, and enjoying each other's company. She noticed the mothers most of all, and the kind and protective way they watched over their children. A woman in a pink baseball cap wiped spaghetti off her son's chin. Another mother spoon-fed her baby with one hand while she lovingly stroked her daughter's hair with the other. She thought about her own mother and tried not to be sad. It wasn't easy.

At least she had her dad. He made her happy.

"You didn't tell them it was my birthday, did you?" she asked him, even though she knew the answer to the question.

"No, of course not," said Terry.

***

But in fact he *had* told their perky, red-haired waitress when he excused himself to go to the bathroom.

Miranda looked at him, unconvinced. "You're lying. You told them."

He knew she could always tell when he was lying, so there was no point in denying it. "They'll give you a free dessert."

"Yeah, and they'll sing 'Happy Birthday' and make a big deal about it."

"What's wrong with that? It's your birthday. It is a big deal."

"Not to me. It's just a birthday. Everyone has them."

Terry wished she weren't so cynical. He wished she had the innocent excitement most kids had on their birthdays. But she wasn't most kids. She had Hannah for a mother.

Miranda observed a young mother holding her son's hand as they passed by their table. "Do you think Mom will ever get better?" she asked.

"Yes, I do," he answered, without hesitating. Hesitation would indicate that he was unsure of his answer. "Your mother used to be perfectly normal. She was a wonderful woman. So full of life. Everyone loved her."

"Yeah, and all that changed when I was born," she said.

Terry didn't know what to say. She was right and he couldn't bullshit her.

"You know, honey, sometimes when mommies have babies, things can get messed up in their brains. It has nothing to do with you. They have medication you can take for it, but your mother hasn't gotten to the point where she wants to do that. But she will. Someday, she will."

"When? I want to have friends over but she never lets me. And she won't let me go to their houses, either. Everyone thinks I hate them."

"I'm sorry, honey. I've been working on her. I'm going to get her help so our family can go back to normal and you'll see what a wonderful mother she is."

She wasn't buying it, he realized. It was only making her sadder.

Miranda reached for a breadstick, took a bite, and scrunched up her face. "These breadsticks taste funny."

Terry reached for one and also took a bite. "You're right. I think they're stale. I'll ask our waitress to bring us some more."

He scanned the room for their perky waitress, the one who swore she'd be right back to take their order, but hadn't been seen since. Frustrated, he looked for someone else to assist them. That's when he spotted a familiar face.

It was Kevin. He was wearing a neatly pressed dress shirt with the top button undone. And no tie. The first thing that struck Terry was how relaxed he appeared. His hair was styled differently and there were no visible sweat stains under his armpits. He even looked like he had lost some weight. Terry felt a tinge of jealousy. He never thought it possible that he could be jealous of Kevin.

"Kevin?" Terry called out.

Kevin turned in Terry's direction, but took a second before he recognized him. Then he flashed a big toothy grin.

"Terry?" Kevin said, as he made his way toward his table with a self-assured gait.

"Kevin. So good to see you," he said, as he read the pin attached to his shirt. "Manager?"

"Yup," replied Kevin, proudly flicking his pin with his right thumb. "I was driving home the day I got let go when I saw a sign from God. It said, 'Now Hiring. Manager. Apply Inside.' Well, I hightailed it in here and applied on the spot. First thing I told them in the interview was, 'No ties.' And, what do ya know? They still hired me. I told you the Lord would provide."

"Yes, you did."

There was an awkward moment as both men smiled at each other, saying nothing. Terry struggled to think of what to say next and nothing came to mind. It was clear to Terry that they never had anything in common but work.

"Could we have some more breadsticks?" said Miranda, breaking the uncomfortable silence. "These taste stale."

Kevin turned his head toward Miranda, noticing her for the first time. "Miranda. Gosh, you look older."

"She is," said Terry, proudly. "Turned eight today."

"Well, I'll be a sonofagun. Happy Birthday! We'll have to do something special for you. Maybe a cake."

Miranda kicked Terry under the table.

"No, that's okay," he quickly interjected. "She doesn't want any fuss, if that's okay."

"Fine. No fuss it is."

Kevin turned back to Terry. "It's good to see you. We should meet for lunch sometime. Catch up."

"That'd be nice," Terry said, knowing it'd never happen.

Miranda slid the bowl of breadsticks toward the edge of the table.

"Okay, then. I'll go get you some more breadsticks. It sure is good to see you again, Terry."

"You, too," managed Terry.

Terry watched Kevin walk away. He'd never thought it possible that Kevin could ever be anything but a person to be pitied. Now it was like he was watching an entirely different person walk away—a person who had altered the course of his life for the better. Seeing Kevin, something dawned on Terry. Life really could change.

Chapter Twenty-Five
Are You Coming In or Not?

Terry had just placed the bouquet of wildflowers next to the hardware store's scuffed-up door when he heard the familiar voice.

"That's funny. It's usually me who does the stalking."

He turned around so fast he nearly lost his balance. There was Renee, positioned with her left cowboy boot propped up on the first step. She looked different to him. Still beautiful, but an unmistakable sadness emanated from her eyes. And a hardness in her face he hadn't seen before.

"I didn't hear you drive up," he said, trying to catch his breath.

"I don't drive. Stud-Muffin, remember? We don't make a lot of noise. That's why I was so good at it."

He leaned against the door to catch his balance. "Good at what?"

"Stalking. Didn't do it all the time. Just to the ones who got under my skin. I had to see what they had that was so much better than me."

"So what did you usually find?" he asked.

"A perfect life," she said, as she pulled her hair back in a ponytail.

"If it was so perfect, why did they do it, then?"

She bounded up the porch's two wooden steps and stopped a few feet from where he was leaning. "Beats the shit out of me. You're a man. You tell me."

There was an edgy, unsettling tenor to her voice that unnerved him. It was like he was talking to a new person.

Someone he barely recognized. "I wouldn't know. I don't cheat."

"Yeah, I know," she said. "You told me."

He had to ask—"Did you stalk me?"

"No."

"Why not? Didn't I get under your skin?"

"You were different. I don't know why. Maybe I respected you enough not to."

"Well... thank you. I guess."

She stared at him for a moment, shaking her head up and down as if answering a question that she hadn't been asked.

"My mother. She liked you. That's why she tried to warn you."

"Warn me? About what?"

"About me. I heard her that day. Telling you to stay away from me."

His eyes dropped to the planked porch. "I didn't listen."

"Yeah, you did," she said. "You've been away for a long time."

He nodded his head in reluctant agreement. "I guess we both have."

"Me and Stud-Muffin ride by here once in a while."

"Yeah, me too," he confessed. "And then one day I decided to come back, but you weren't here. Your friend Otis told me what happened."

"Otis isn't a friend," she quickly corrected him. Then she looked down at the flowers he'd left by the door. "Are these for me or my mother?"

"Actually," he said, "they're for both of you."

"Poppies," she said, as she reached down and picked up the flowers. "They were her favorite." She added, quietly, "Mine, too." She smiled slightly and then inserted her key into the lock. "Now, if you'll excuse me, I've got a little business to take care of."

He watched disconsolately as she struggled to turn the key in the resistant old latch. When it finally gave way, she yanked out the keys and gave the door a swift kick with her boot.

He couldn't leave now. Not like this. There was too much he wanted to say.

"Mind if I come in?"

"Don't know," she said, as she turned around to look at him. "You lied to me."

"Lied to you? When?"

She leaned against the frame of the door. "I saw you 'bout a week ago. I was riding past Home Despot and there you were in the parking lot loading a bunch of packages into your trunk. You promised me you'd never go back there."

"I'm sorry. I needed some things. And you weren't open."

"Fair enough. Just don't let it happen again."

She let the door slam behind her and disappeared into the store. Terry stood on the porch listening to her scuffling around as she switched on a few lights.

And then he heard her voice.

"Well? Are you coming in or not?"

Chapter Twenty-Six
Never to Ring Again

Terry walked into the hardware store. He couldn't see Renee at first, but he could smell her. It wasn't perfume, because she didn't wear any. It was an earthy aroma her body naturally produced that he had never smelled on a woman before. Subtle, yet instantly recognizable. Fierce, yet feminine. Untamed, yet vulnerable. Every time he smelled it, he wanted to capture it, harness it, and own it. He wanted to breathe it in and be one with it. He longed for the day when he could taste it. He knew it would happen one day, and that day was getting closer and closer. It might even be today.

***

Renee stood behind the counter, just as she had on the first day he entered the store, watching in the convex security mirror as he maneuvered through the aisles toward her like a mouse in a maze. He looked nothing like that first day she saw him. Back then, he was tightly wound, distant, and distracted. He seemed more focused now. And confident.

"Are these flowers from your property?" she asked, as he cleared the corner and made his way to the counter. He looked taller than she remembered. Or maybe he was just standing up straighter.

"Yes," he replied.

She loved the way he said "yes." It sounded so proper. Most of the men she knew said "yup" or "yeah" or "uh-huh." He said "yes."

"They're real nice," she said, setting the flowers on the counter as if they were made of delicate glass. "Grab one of those vases from aisle three for me, would ya? I want to get them in some water."

He turned around, halted, and then said, "Where's aisle three?"

"If you count from the right, it's the third one in. About halfway down on the left-hand side."

She watched in the mirror as he searched for the shelf and she smiled. He was standing right by them but he didn't see them. *Some things never change*, she thought.

"On the top shelf," she said.

He looked up, quickly grabbed one, and then rushed back to her as if making up for lost time.

"There's only a few left," he informed her, as he placed the vase on the counter. "Might want to order some more."

"I'm not ordering anything ever again for this place," she said, as she carefully guided the stems into the shallow opening of the vase.

"Why?" he asked.

She stood back and admired the flowers. "Nice to have some life back in here." They weren't perfectly arranged, but she didn't care. Some things were more beautiful when left alone.

She took the vase into the bathroom and began to fill it with water.

She had heard his question. She just chose not to answer. She was reluctant to say she was thinking of selling the store. It was one thing to be ruminating about something in her head, but to reveal that decision to someone else gave it a finality that she wasn't ready to express.

***

He wondered why she didn't answer his question, but he knew she had a reason. She wasn't one to avoid a direct question. If she didn't answer, it was because she chose not to.

"How long were you shut down?"

"Long enough to realize I didn't miss it," she said, returning from the bathroom. "I'm putting it on the market on Monday."

"You're selling?" he asked, unable to conceal the disappointment in his voice.

She placed the flowers on the corner of the counter next to the cash register and then walked down the hall to her office and went inside.

Terry quickly followed her. When he reached the door, she was crouched down behind her desk, rummaging through her bottom drawer. "Why?"

"I hate this place. Always have."

"But it just seems to be a part of who you are."

"Yeah, the bad part."

"I don't understand," he said. He didn't like this new attitude of hers. She was moving on and he didn't want her to. He didn't know where moving on left him.

He began to enter the office.

"Don't come in here," she said, standing upright.

"Okay," he replied, confused. "Do you want me to leave?"

"No, I just don't want you to get hurt."

"Get hurt?"

And then he saw it. She was holding a handgun.

"What the hell are you doing?" he asked, panicked.

"I told you, I have a little business to take care of." Then she aimed at the sofa, her hand steady, and cocked the gun. "Something I should have done years ago."

Without flinching, she fired off a succession of shots. Bullet holes penetrated the cushions and stuffing started spurting from the sofa, floating around the room like soiled snowflakes.

Terry ducked into the hall and watched through the crack of the door as she continued her shooting spree, a steely gaze in her eyes. She fired again and again until the sofa was obliterated beyond recognition, like Bonnie and Clyde's car after the posse of police officers riddled it with a hundred and thirty rounds when one or two would have sufficed.

When the final round was shot, she brushed an errant strand of hair from her face and calmly placed the gun on the desk.

"You can come in now. I'm done."

He didn't move.

"What the hell? What did you do that for?" he asked through the crack in the door.

She slowly lowered herself onto her chair as a tiny speck of sofa stuffing settled on the top of her head.

"My dad was a former hippie," she began. "Free love and all that shit. Then, eventually, like all of 'em, he had to get a job. So he borrowed money from his grandpa and bought this store. Changed the name to 'Hardware California.' Get it? Like the song 'Hotel California'? "

Terry cautiously came out from behind the door, but remained in the hall.

She took a deep breath and continued.

"That's where he used to take me," she said, indicating the bullet-riddled sofa. "Couldn't stand looking at it anymore. I don't know why I ever kept it. Should have killed it years ago. Right after he croaked."

Terry thought he misheard her. "Take you?"

"Molest me," she clarified, bluntly.

His face drained of color. It was not what he was expecting to hear. "Renee. I'm so…"

"No. Don't say you're sorry. I don't want your pity. I hate that."

He couldn't believe what he was hearing. "How old were you?"

"Twelve. That's when it got real bad. He did shit before that, but twelve is when he…"

"My God, Renee… did you ever tell your mother?"

"Didn't have to. She knew. That's why she hated me. And I hated her for not stopping it."

Terry took a step into the room. "Have you ever told anyone this? Besides me?"

"No. You're the only one. Lucky you."

"I don't know what to say."

"You don't have to say anything. There's nothing to say. What's done is done." She leaned forward in her chair. "Now it's your turn to tell me something."

"What do you mean?" he asked.

"You can tell me your secret. You're hiding something, too. I can't put my finger on it, but there's something you're not telling me. I had this feeling since the day we met."

"I don't know what you're talking about."

"Bullshit. I'm very perceptive. You can't keep it from me. Not after what I told you."

"I never asked you to."

"So, you're just going to leave me hanging here? I tell you something I've never told anyone else… and you're going to continue to hide your secret? What is it, huh? Are you gay?"

"No," he said unequivocally. "What would make you think that?"

"I don't know. You're not like other guys. More sensitive. You're married, but you're obviously not having sex."

"How do you know that? I never told you that."

"Didn't have to," she said. "I'm a woman. We can sense those things. I can smell an unsatisfied man a mile away."

"Well, you're wrong."

"I don't think I am. You can admit it, you know," she said, standing up. "You can admit that you hate your life, your marriage, your wife."

"I told you I don't hate my wife!" he screamed out, abruptly. "I loved her!"

"*Loved* her?" she asked. "So you don't love her anymore?"

"That's not what I meant. I meant to say that I love her."

"Then why are you here?"

"I don't know. It was a mistake. I should have never come back."

Renee kicked her chair back against the wall and stormed over to Terry. "Then get the hell out!"

Terry began to gradually back away.

"I mean it this time. And don't come back."

Terry could see that she was deadly serious.

"But do me a favor, will ya?" she said, her voice low and lethal. "Fix whatever is wrong with you or your marriage or whatever you got going on, but do it quick before you screw up your daughter even further than you already have. She deserves better."

He stood there like a dutiful school boy waiting for his teacher to finish scolding him.

"Now get out," she said resolutely.

He hesitated for a moment, and then turned around and walked out of her life.

***

Renee stood frozen in place, wondering where it all went wrong. He was leaving. Forever. She could stop him. There was still time.

And then she heard the bell ring as he walked out of the hardware store for the last and final time. She heard him start his car and begin to pull out of the parking lot. He was going slower than usual, almost beckoning her to run out and stop him. But she stayed put, determined to resist the temptation to chase after a relationship that was doomed from the beginning. There was no point. It was over.

When she could no longer hear his car, she looked down and spotted her gun lying on the desk. A sudden thought entered her mind. She grabbed it abruptly and pressed the release, causing the empty magazine to drop out of its grip and land with a thud on a pile of unpaid bills. She reached in her bottom drawer and removed a loaded magazine and inserted it into the gun. *Click!* Then she charged down the hall. When she reached the entrance of the store, she took direct aim at the bell and blasted it off its mount. *Bang!*

It was finally silenced. Never to ring again.

Part Three

Chapter Twenty-Seven
Her Mother Would Never Understand

Renee loved her father. He wasn't like her mother; he was the fun one. The one who let her break the rules. She could do anything she wanted around him and nothing was off limits, nothing was taboo. She could cuss, stay up late, skip school, drink, and even take a hit off his "peace" pipe once in awhile. There was one rule, though—she couldn't tell anybody what they did.

Her mother, on the other hand, was all about rules. She made Renee wear dresses, speak correct English, do her homework, and even go to church every Sunday. She insisted that she help out around the store, tend to her horse, and respect authority, even if she didn't agree with it.

So when her father began sexually abusing her, Renee went along with it. Because her mother taught her to respect authority, even if she didn't agree with it.

The first time he touched her "down there" was when she was eight years old, but the abuse began way before that day. Of course, it didn't seem like abuse at the time. It seemed like love. He was grooming her like a horse. He was always telling her how beautiful she was, and how special she was, and how much she meant to him. He told her how they had a bond that no one could ever break.

He began to tell her things she had to swear to secrecy. Things she could never tell anyone else, especially not her mother. Renee dutifully obeyed. She loved the fact that he trusted her and treated her like an adult; unlike her mother, who was always treating her like a child. She hated that. She hated being a child. She'd dream that she was eighteen and could do whatever she wanted. She told her father this and he said that she could be whatever age she wanted to be. He said that just because society told you what age you were didn't mean you had to act that way.

So when the abuse began, she told herself that she was eighteen and that made it okay.

She was in the supply room the first time it happened.

She had just finished organizing the shelves and wanted to show her father how good of a job she'd done. Even though it was her mother who asked her to do the task, it was her father she wanted to impress the most. And besides, her mother wasn't at the store. She was gone doing errands. Her mother was always doing errands.

She made him close his eyes because she wanted it to be a surprise. When she finally told him to look and see, his face lit up as he scanned the room and saw everything she had done. He was very impressed. So impressed that he gave her a big kiss on the lips. He had never kissed her that way before, so she knew that she had done a really good job. And then he took her in his arms and gave her a hug; one that seemed to last forever. Now she really knew she had done a good job.

She couldn't see him because her face was pressed up against his chest, but she could feel his heart beating rapidly beneath his blue flannel shirt, the one with the buttons that snapped. She told him once how much she loved that shirt. Since then, he wore it almost every day.

He picked her up and he spun her around. She started getting dizzy, but she didn't want to tell him to stop because she didn't want to hurt his feelings. As they were spinning, he grabbed her behind and squeezed it. And then she felt his finger lifting up her dress. She thought that his finger would stop when it reached her underwear, but it didn't. It kept going—under the elastic, and then higher, until it reached the area where she peed.

And even though he stopped spinning her, his hand didn't stop moving. Rubbing. Caressing. And then entering.

It hurt and she cried out, but he buried her face deeper into his chest to muffle the sound.

She didn't like what he was doing, but she couldn't tell him to stop. He seemed so happy at the job she'd done. He was just trying to show her how appreciative he was. So she let him. It seemed like it would never end.

When he was done, she didn't feel eight anymore.

This went on for four years. And then, when she was twelve, he took it to the next level. He penetrated her with his penis.

And on that day, a part of Renee died.

When he was finished, he told her that she was a big girl now and that big girls had secrets. This was a secret she could never tell anyone. Especially her mother, he said. He told her that her mother would never understand.

Deep down, she knew he was right. Her mother would never understand.

Chapter Twenty-Eight
Let's Get the Hell Out of Here

Etched into Lois Patrick's modest, maroon-colored gravestone was her full name, date of birth, and date of death. Renee couldn't come up with a concise, cutesy quote that adequately captured her mother's philosophy, so she decided to stick with the facts.

Clutching Terry's flowers tightly in her hands, Renee knelt down on the sparse grass surrounding the gravesite. She set the flowers at the base of the stone, and then traced her fingers along the embossed letters' edges. She still couldn't believe her mother was gone forever. Renee had always hoped that someday they'd have that "talk," that "clearing of the air," and everything would go back to the way it was.

But that hope ended on the day she returned to the hardware store and discovered her mother lying on the cold, hard concrete floor behind the counter, her mouth agape in frozen protest, her hand clamped onto her left breast. Her eyes had been wide open, staring at Renee. Staring at nothing.

"You'll never guess who these are from," she said, as she struggled not to cry. She wouldn't allow herself. She was already cried out. No more. No more.

"Terry Boyle. But you knew that already, didn't you? You know everything now. Just like God. You know everything that's happening. That's *happened*."

She paused a moment.

"I miss you, Mom. I don't have any friends anymore. You were my only one. Women hate me. Men use me. They always have. Starting with Dad."

She could see her reflection in the polished slab of marble. She looked tired, old, and more like her mother than she ever had.

"I have something I want to ask you. I wish I would have asked you when you were alive, but I was afraid. Afraid your answer wouldn't satisfy me. How could it? What could you say? How could you possibly justify your silence? But I want to know. I need to know, Mother."

She took a deep breath and looked up at the sky. The clouds were swirling and the sky was turning dark.

"If you knew about it, why didn't you do anything to stop him? Huh, Lois? You were my mother. You were supposed to protect me. But instead you ran away. I hated you for that. I feel like I still hate you. I don't want to. I want to just let it go, but I can't.

"Were you mad at me for letting him? I was just a kid and he was my father. He wasn't supposed to hurt me. He was a sick fuck and we both knew it. Is he up there? I hope not. I hope he's rotting in hell. He ruined my life and I hate him for it.

"What should I do now? Huh, Mother? Should I sell the store? Do you want me to keep it? You want me to, don't you? You hated it as much as I did, but we couldn't seem to walk away from it. It was a part of us. There were a lot of bad memories there, but lots of good ones, too."

She picked up the flowers and started gently caressing the petals of the poppies between her fingers.

"Do you know what I miss about you the most, Mother? The before. When I was young. We used to go to church together every Sunday and every holy day. Just you and me. Dad never came. He said he was spiritual but not religious. Turns out he was just plain evil.

"But then we stopped going. I know why now. It was after you found out. You lost your faith. I don't blame you. But I wish you would have stuck with it. With me. I felt safe when we were alone together. I haven't felt that safe since. I just want to feel safe again."

She could no longer control the tears. They flowed unabashedly down her face despite her failed attempts to wipe them away with the back of her hand. She hated feeling like this. Sad, hurt, angry. She could barely deal with one of these emotions, much less all of them descending on her simultaneously.

"Why, Mom, why?" she said, thrusting the flowers forward to accentuate each word she said. "Why did you abandon me? I hate you for what you did! I hate you!"

As her anger intensified, she smacked the wildflowers against the jagged edge on top of the gravestone.

"Maybe you're not in heaven. Maybe you're in hell with Dad. You are both to blame for what happened to me! It's true. You may not want to hear this, but you have no choice. You can't shut me up. You can't make me feel silly. Or dirty. Or guilty. Not anymore."

She hurled what remained of the battered bouquet on the ground next to the grave.

Just then, a droplet of moisture struck her on the top of her head. She turned her head toward the stormy sky. She knew she had to get out of there before the downpour hit. Stud-Muffin didn't like the rain. Neither did she, for that matter.

Without looking back at the grave, she ran to Stud-Muffin and thrust herself onto the saddle. "C'mon, boy," she said, as she lightly kicked his muscular sides. "Let's get the hell out of here."

Chapter Twenty-Nine
You're Already Halfway There

"You're cheating on me, aren't you?" Hannah accused Terry the minute he arrived home.

"No, Hannah, I'm not cheating on you," he said, as he brushed past her.

He was in no mood for a fight. It had been a long day. Two more despondent clients had come in to drop their insurance. One had been with him for more than ten years.

"I don't believe you," she said, following closely behind him. "Where were you? It's past ten o'clock."

"I told you I'd be working late. It's just me and Wayne left." He added, "And Karen."

"Is it Karen?" she asked, as she removed the seal from a fresh pack of cigarettes. "That who you been screwing?"

"Let's not do this tonight. I've had a long day and I'm exhausted. Did Miranda go to sleep okay?"

"Don't change the subject. And you didn't deny it."

"What are you talking about?"

"Karen! Are you having an affair with Karen?"

"No," he said. "That's ridiculous." He opened the fridge. There was hardly anything in it, which reminded him that he forgot to get groceries on his way home.

"Aren't you happy with me?" she asked. She inserted a cigarette between her lips. "I'm happy with you."

He slammed the refrigerator door shut, causing the magnet holding up one of Miranda's school art projects to pop off and spring through the air.

"You're happy? You certainly don't look happy to me!" Terry shouted, unable to contain his anger any longer.

Hannah dropped to the floor as if she'd been struck. "I want to be happy! But I'm not! I can't help it!" she cried as she picked up the artwork from the floor. It was a collage Miranda had constructed for a book report assignment.

"It's because you've given up!" he said, snatching the collage out of her hands.

But she held on, causing the paper to rip in half.

For a moment, they stood staring at their respective pieces. Finally, Terry said, "I'll tape it up tomorrow."

"She'll know."

"No, she won't. I'll see to it." He grabbed the severed piece from her hand and began to leave the room.

"I saw the phone bill," she said, standing up. There was an eerie resonance in her tone.

Terry stopped. "What?"

"The phone bill. Didn't think I'd catch it, did you?"

"What are you talking about?"

"There was a number I didn't recognize. Someone called it three times. It wasn't me. I was curious, so I called it."

He slowly turned around and faced her.

Her eyes were searing into his. "An institution? For psychos? You trying to get me committed?"

"No," he said, "I'm trying to get you help. And it's not an institution. It's a treatment center."

She began to walk menacingly toward him. "You'll never put me in one of those loony bins, surrounded by stiffs in lab coats and pill cups and needles and beds with straps on them. I've got rights. I'm not some kid. I can refuse and there's nothing you can do about it."

Terry narrowed his eyes. "You know," he said. "I think I'm beginning to see that. There's nothing I can do about it. I'm through trying to help."

"Through? What does that mean?"

But he didn't answer.

"If you leave me," she whispered hoarsely, "I'll kill myself. I swear to God."

He began to ascend the stairs. "You're already halfway there."

Chapter Thirty
Peace

Renee took a deep breath and reached for the iron handles on the ornate wooden church door. They were just as heavy and hard to open as she remembered from when she was a little girl. Some things never got easier.

The Mass was already in progress. She quickly sat down in the last pew. A man with a thick German accent was doing the second reading and she couldn't understand a word he was saying. She tuned him out and began looking around at all the familiar surroundings instead. Nothing seemed to have changed since the last time she entered those hefty doors so many years ago with her mother. The gilded crosses still adorned the high arched ceiling. The oversized chandeliers encased in iron, the ones she used to fear would fall and crush her in the event of an earthquake, still hung suspended from the wooden beams. The finely detailed life-sized statues of the saints retained their frozen, timeless expressions. The only one she could identify by name was St. Francis, because he loved animals. All the rest looked sad to her.

No, nothing had changed but the priest and the people. She didn't recognize anyone from where she was sitting. The men she slept with were most likely in the front row with their wives and their children.

She stood up, along with the throng of parishioners, as the priest approached the podium to read from the Gospel. She remembered this part. As always, he began with the timeless greeting, "The Lord be with you." She knew by heart what came next; some things you never forget. "And also with you," she responded.

But it wasn't what everyone else replied. She couldn't hear what they said, but it had the word "spirit" in it. She felt her face flush with blood as the people around her turned her way. Had they heard her? She thought she had whispered it. But obviously they had heard, because they were all looking at her. Most were smiling but some were not. She tried to block them out by blurring her vision so she couldn't make out anyone's faces.

So, apparently, things had changed. Now they were saying different words. All at once, she felt like an outsider and all she wanted to do was bolt out of there. But she knew if she did that, everyone would stare at her again. She wasn't used to feeling self-conscious. She prided herself on her "I don't give a crap what anyone thinks of me" attitude; her ability to be herself at all times, in all situations, and to hell with those who didn't like it or her.

But church was different. Church made her feel like a child all over again. And she didn't like that feeling. Being a child the first time around was bad enough.

She decided to leave, but waited patiently for the most inconspicuous opportunity. She found her chance when everyone was sitting back down to listen to the homily—but someone stopped her.

It was a little girl with unruly blonde hair and brown soulful eyes. She was with her mother, sitting two rows in front of Renee. She turned around and smiled. It was a commiserative smile.

Renee smiled at her and then decided to stay.

The priest's homily was about redemption, forgiveness, and salvation—something Renee desperately needed to hear that Sunday. She felt that the priest was speaking directly to her—like he was reading her mind. She blocked out all the people around her—the ones wondering why she was late, why she was sweating under her armpits, why they hadn't seen her before, why she hadn't bothered to wear any makeup, why she didn't know the correct words to say. All she focused on were the words the priest was saying. They were different from the words she used to hear as a young girl. They were harsher back then. *Blaspheme. Repentance. Sinful. Deceit.* Sure, the Mass may have changed, but so had the tone. It was kinder. *Renewal. Acceptance. Absolution. Love.* And as she listened intently to the words, she began to feel a sensation she hadn't felt in a long time.

Peace.

Chapter Thirty-One
Ready to Let Go

Renee used to love attending Mass, but always hated going to confession. She didn't understand why she couldn't just tell her sins directly to God. Why did she have to go through a priest? Her mother explained that priests were a fast track to heaven, but she never bought that one.

There was another reason she didn't like going to confession. She knew that whatever sin she confessed, no matter how bad it was, the priests were sworn to secrecy and couldn't tell another living soul. There was only one instance in which they were compelled to reveal what had been confessed to them—if a crime had been committed.

So when she was a little girl, she wouldn't utter a word about what her father was doing to her. Not to anyone, and certainly not to a priest. They might throw her father in jail and probably her, too. She was, after all, just as guilty as he was. And what would her mother do if she found out? Would she believe her? Would she scold her? Even worse, would she abandon her? Send her to foster care?

No, it was better to keep it in.

But now she knew better. Her father was the criminal, not her. And now that he was dead, there was nothing the priest could do or say about it.

So why, then, was she about to tell her terrible little secret to a priest after all these years? Renee didn't know the answer. All she knew was that she needed to tell someone besides Terry. Telling him helped temporarily, but it did nothing to alleviate the anger she still fostered in her heart. Not so much directed at her father, but at her mother.

Renee sat patiently waiting for her turn to confess. Each time a parishioner entered the tiny booth with a small cross affixed to the door, a red light went on indicating that they had knelt down and begun baring his or her soul.

Two priests, serving as conduits to Christ, were on duty—tucked away in their respective confessionals, listening attentively, and eventually doling out what they deemed fair penances for each sinner's transgressions. Renee leaned forward slightly, trying to make out what was being said, but all she heard was mumbling, whispering, and some sniffles. Some people took only a few minutes and some seemed to take forever.

She had no idea how long she'd take or what she'd end up confessing. Perhaps she'd chicken out and just revert to the basics such as lying, cussing, having impure thoughts—the things that everyone copped to because they weren't as scandalous as other sins.

Or maybe she'd go into detail about what she'd done, and with whom, and give the poor priest a heart attack.

She gazed up at the statue of Jesus hanging on the cross behind the altar looming down on her. She'd always detested the depiction of a lifeless half-naked Jesus, his thorny-crowned head hanging low, blood frozen in mid-seep from a wound in his side. It was too realistic for her taste. She preferred the ones where Jesus's arms were raised to the heavens in anticipation of His ascension. She liked to be reminded of what happened to Him *after* He was crucified—that all the cruelty and suffering He endured was ultimately worth it.

She sensed someone looking at her. She turned her head and saw that it was the little girl who'd been sitting two rows in front of her during Mass. She wondered what such a young girl would have to confess. But then she remembered the secret she kept inside at her age. She couldn't bear to think that what had happened to her could possibly ever happen to anyone else. But deep down, she knew it happened to little girls and boys every day. She knew it would never end. She knew there would always be evil in this world.

Renee tipped her head and smiled. The little girl smiled back.

A middle-aged man with a look of relief on his face exited one of the confessionals and went directly back into the church, knelt down, and began to say his penance.

The girl's mother was next. She entered the confessional and closed the door behind her. Moments later, the little girl slid down the pew next to Renee and whispered, "Don't go in the one my mom went in. It's Father Carter. He's mean."

Renee shook her head and mouthed the word, "Okay."

"The other priest—Father Moberg—is nice," the little girl continued. "And old. So, he may die before he has a chance to tell anyone."

Renee leaned over to the girl. "They're not supposed to tell."

"You don't really believe that, do you? What do you think the priests talk about at dinner with each other? It's not like they have a family. They're only human, you know."

Renee couldn't believe how mature this little girl was. So wise. And articulate. Just like Renee had been at that age.

"Are you afraid?" the little girl asked.

"No," Renee said.

"You look afraid."

Renee looked down at her hands. They were trembling. "It's just been a long time and I have a lot to confess."

"Don't be afraid," she said. "You don't have to tell them *every*thing, you know."

The little girl quickly snapped her head up when she heard her mother exiting the confessional, and then moved away.

Renee watched the little girl walk boldly toward the beckoning door.

"I'm Renee, by the way," she whispered loudly after her. "What's your name?"

But the little girl didn't hear her. She had already shut the door and triggered the red light.

Renee clasped her hands together, put her head down, and prayed. She prayed for the little girl. She prayed for herself. She prayed for all the little children in the world living with a secret.

And then she heard the door to the confessional open. It was her turn.

Renee stood up. She was ready. Ready to let go.

Chapter Thirty-Two
What Is It?

Father Moberg thought he'd heard everything. He'd been ordained in 1963 and over the years he'd listened to countless confessions. It had taken some adjustment in the beginning to hear people confess their deepest, darkest secrets, but he had always been a good listener and it didn't take long for him to settle into one of the requisites of his job.

The worst part was when he recognized the voice, which was most of the time. It was hard not being distracted while discussing fundraising with Mrs. Havelston, president of the Parish Women's Council, after she confessed that she fantasized about having sexual relations with her husband's boss. Or having dinner with Mr. and Mrs. Micholson, when he knew Mr. Micholson was fornicating with his secretary. Or looking down from the pulpit at little Jimmy Rotella in the front row, sandwiched between his parents, the picture of innocence, and knowing he had felt up little Sally McMann on the bus after a field trip to the local community theater's production of *The Music Man*.

Over time, he listened not so much to the words, but the way they were said. He learned to listen to the pain, the sorrow, and the remorse so he could focus on doling out a penance that was both fair and appropriate in order for them to feel good about themselves for a brief moment and then go out and continue to sin. They, like him, were only human, after all.

The woman began hesitantly. "I don't know what I'm doing here."

"You're here to make a confession to God," he replied.

"I know that," she explained. "I meant that I didn't expect to be doing this. Not yet."

Father Moberg paused a moment. "Shall we begin?" he asked.

"Sure," she said. "Do *I* begin or do you? It's been a long time since I've gone to confession."

"Why don't I begin, and then you just say what comes to mind."

"Okay, I can do that," she said.

"In the name of the Father, and of the Son, and of the Holy Spirit," Father Moberg recited, and then he waited for her response.

After an uncomfortable silence, she said, "Am I supposed to say something?"

"Yes—Amen."

"Oh. Yeah. Amen. Now what?"

"Well, you can begin by telling me how long it's been since your last confession, and then you can just start."

"My last confession? Jesus. Let me think."

He could hear her mumbling to herself as she tried to compute the answer in her head.

"It doesn't really matter. What matters is that you're here. You can just—"

"—Twenty-six years!" she blurted out. "Sorry. Took me a while to do the math. Been a long time, huh?"

"It doesn't matter. What's important is that you're here today."

Father Moberg could hear her shift in her chair as she leaned closer to the mesh separating them. "Before we start, can I make a little suggestion?"

"Of course," Father Moberg replied.

"I think you should have some hitching posts in the parking lot. This is still a rural community at heart and even though they have all these fancy places popping up all over the place like Starbucks and shit—sorry, I meant, stuff—there's still a lot of folks who ride horses and there's nowhere to hitch 'em. I had to walk a mile just to get here. And it made me late for Mass. Everyone was looking at me. Sweat pouring down my face. I felt like a greasy pig. Put on my best blouse for nothing."

"I'm sorry about that. I'll take it up with the council members."

"It'd bring in a lot more folks, don't ya think?" she continued. "You gotta be hurting for business, what with all those pervert priests coming out of the woodwork. I hate perverts. Not that you're one. You seem really nice."

"Thank you. Now, would you like to begin?"

"Are you in a hurry?"

"Yeah, I've got a hot date tonight."

"A sense of humor," she said, and laughed. "I like that in a man." She caught herself. "I mean, a priest."

"I'm a man, and a priest."

"That's good to know."

***

There was so much to tell. So much that she'd been keeping inside and wanted to get off her chest. She was ready to start anew, and if she didn't unload all of it at once, she'd never feel free.

But first...

"Did you change the Mass? They changed the way we used to say things. Like 'and with your spirit.' What's that all about? I thought the Mass was the one thing I could count on to stay the same."

"Yes, a few years back we changed some things. I can give you a pamphlet about it when you're done."

"No, that's okay. I'll catch on. If I come back."

"Well," he said, encouragingly, "I sure hope you do."

"I'll think about it. Maybe you won't want me to after what I'm about to tell you."

"I can assure you, nothing you can say to me will change my opinion of you. You are a child of God and should be loved as such. Everyone deserves that. Now, if you'd like to begin."

His words comforted her, so she decided to tell him. Everything.

She began by telling him that her father had sexually abused her starting when she was eight years old. She waited for him to gasp or react in some shocked way, but all he said was, "Go on."

She went on to tell him about her promiscuous teenage years, her affairs with married men and then, finally, her anger at her mother. Almost a half hour passed before she finally concluded with, "I guess that's all." And then she let out a heavy sigh. "That took a long time. I'm sorry. Hogging up all the time for the others, huh?"

But he didn't respond. In fact, he hadn't said a word the entire time she was confessing.

"Excuse me?" she said through the screen. "Are you going to say anything or do I just leave? I thought you were supposed to give me some prayers to say or something, from what I remember, or did that part change, too? Am I beyond hope? I mean, I thought if I confessed my sins I'd be forgiven."

"I assure you. You are forgiven," he stated.

"Thank God," she said, and she exhaled loudly.

"But there's something else I feel I must tell you, even though I am not supposed to."

There was a long pause before she asked, "What is it?"

Chapter Thirty-Three
I Forgive You, Mom

Father Moberg was old enough to know the rules, but in this case he said to hell with it. Some rules were made to be broken.

"I've never met you, but I know who you are because of the things you've told me, the names you've mentioned, and the terrible sin perpetrated on you by your sick father.

"You see, I knew your mother."

He gave her a minute to respond, hoping she'd say something, anything that signified he should continue, but he only heard the sad and eerie sound of her slow, measured breathing.

"Your mother came to confession quite frequently. Twice a month, sometimes. And she always talked about the same thing. Even though I told her that God had forgiven her, she kept coming back. She said she couldn't believe that God would ever forgive her for what she did, or rather what she didn't do. Your mother lived with terrible guilt for not stopping the abuse.

"I urged her to talk with you about it but she said that you'd never forgive her. I told her to at least try, but she just couldn't bring herself to do it. Rather, she kept coming back and asking for forgiveness. The last time she came to me was just a few days before her death. She told me that she believed God had forgiven her, and she was ready to talk to you and beg for your forgiveness. But she never got the chance."

He stopped talking when he thought he heard a sniffle. After a moment of silence, he continued. "Are you okay?"

She didn't answer.

"I read about your mother's death in the paper. Had I known sooner, I would have reached out to you and we could have had a funeral for her here. But you had no way of knowing that she had returned to the church, and it was too late when I learned. She was already buried.

"I can't imagine what a shock it must have been for you. I'm truly sorry for your loss. Your mother was a wonderful woman and I will miss her."

He stopped again, and this time he clearly heard her sniffle. She was crying.

"I want you to know that it's up to you now. You don't have to forgive her. You can hate her until the day you die. But I believe that will only end up hurting you. You have your life to live, and you'll never be able to live it fully until you let go of the past.

"What happened to you was not your fault. How you dealt with it over the years was completely understandable, considering what you'd been through. But that path of life only brought you misery and unhappiness—and anger. You've been released from your sins of the past. Now it's time to let go of the anger."

He was done speaking and he waited for her to talk, but she never did. After a few moments, she opened the door of the confessional and shut it quietly behind her.

He said a quick prayer that someday she'd be back, but he knew she probably wouldn't be. He'd learned a long time ago that not all prayers were answered.

***

Renee knelt at her mother's grave, weeping openly. Stud-Muffin stood staidly at her side, his head bowed a few inches from hers. All she could do was cry, and she did, for what seemed like an eternity. When she was finished, she dried her eyes and said a quick prayer.

Then she looked up at the sky and said, "I forgive you, Mom."

Chapter Thirty-Four
He'd Finally Gotten to It Once and For All

Terry knew that today was the day. He knew it the moment he arrived at work and saw Karen's bloodshot eyes staring at him pitifully over the top of her computer screen. She always knew things before anyone else did.

So it came as no surprise when Wayne called him into his office and regretfully informed him he was being "let go." Terry listened numbly as Wayne rattled off a roster of reasons for his decision. He couldn't make out complete sentences, just certain words such as "cutting back," "downsizing," "reorganizing," "bad economy," etc. All he could think about was his future, his finances, and his family. What the hell would he do now? Insurance was all he knew. He didn't even have a college degree.

The severance package Wayne offered him would barely carry him through the end of the year, so he needed to start looking for work immediately and he didn't even know where to begin. He'd never been in an unemployment line, never filled out a job application, and certainly never been fired from a job.

"I'm so sorry, Mr. Boyle," Karen said tearfully, as she watched Terry pack his belongings in the reusable grocery bags he kept in the trunk of his car.

"Don't be. I had a feeling I was next. Nothing lasts forever."

"Where would you like me to forward your calls?" She was dabbing at her eyes with an embroidered white handkerchief she had hand-stitched. She used to sell them at the office, back when there was still a staff to sell them to.

"To my cell phone, please. I haven't figured out how I'm going to tell Hannah yet."

"I'm going to miss you. It's going to be like a ghost town around here now."

"Not for long. I'm sure he'll hire someone to take my place soon. Probably got someone lined up already. Some fresh, young college kid he can pay a lot less than I got paid. Someone who can learn all these new insurance rules faster than I could."

Karen lumbered over to Terry's desk and picked up the photo of Terry and Hannah at the beach. "What a great picture. You both look so happy."

"Yeah," he said, taking it from her and shoving it in the bag. "It was taken a long time ago."

"Time sure flies, doesn't it?"

"Wait till you get to my age. It moves like a brakeless freight train."

"I don't think I'll make it to your age. Probably won't even make thirty."

"Why would you think that?"

"I don't know. I just always had the feeling I was going to die young. Like Brittany Murphy or Amy Winehouse. I just can't picture myself old."

"Neither could I when I was your age. And then one day you look in the mirror and you barely recognize yourself."

"At least you have a wife and a daughter. I don't have anyone." Terry stopped packing momentarily and looked at her. She was staring at the faded paint imprints where he'd just removed his framed insurance awards. "When I go, I wonder if I'll have made an impression on anyone. If anyone will even remember me."

"Of course they will," he said half-heartedly, as he continued packing.

"No one remembers you unless you're famous."

"That's not true. Your loved ones remember you. And that's all that matters."

She broke her trance-like state and turned to Terry with a giddy look in her eyes. "Do you think I could make it on *The Bachelorette*? I've applied a bunch of times, but I never heard back from them."

"I don't know. I've never seen it."

"Oh my God. Really? You should watch it. It's so good." The phone in the outer office rang. "I'm going to try again. Sooner or later, they have to call, right?"

"Right." He didn't even attempt to sound convincing, as he knew she wasn't listening to a word he said.

She skipped out of the room to answer the phone with a big smile on her face, probably thinking about how cool it would be to get on *The Bachelorette* and become famous. And how it would change her life.

Terry opened the top drawer of his desk and saw Miranda's torn artwork, the two pieces bound together by a paperclip. When Miranda noticed it wasn't magnetized to the refrigerator, he had lied and told her he was so proud of it that he had taken it to the office to show everyone. He kept meaning to repair it, but as usual, he never found the time. Now he had lots of time. He rummaged through the packed grocery bags, and found his tape dispenser. He lined up the two severed pieces and carefully taped the artwork together. Then he turned the picture over and observed his handiwork. From the front, you could never tell that it had been ripped apart.

He began loading the bags in the trunk of his car. They'd remain there until he had worked up the nerve to break the news to Hannah. Who knows, maybe he'd luck out and get a new job before he even had to tell her. Perhaps he'd get a *sign* on the way home like Kevin did.

After he'd loaded the last bag, he did a final surveillance of the room to make sure he'd gotten everything. It was empty. Just as empty as when it had been filled with his things.

He was about to close the door for the last time when he noticed his nameplate hanging on by a thread. He gave the door a good slam shut and the nameplate swayed back and forth before it finally became unhinged and tumbled to the ground. There. He'd finally gotten to it once and for all.

Chapter Thirty-Five
Today is Going to Be a Good Day

Hannah sat at the kitchen table after Terry and Miranda left for the day, reminiscing about the dream she'd had the night before. It was a good dream.

From the time she was a young girl, she had feared oceans, seas, and even lakes—any deep body of water where you couldn't see the bottom. It all stemmed from an incident that happened when she was five years old. She slipped on the deck of her uncle's fishing boat and fell overboard. At first, no one heard her as she screamed for help and thrashed about in the water. She knew how to swim, but panic eradicated her ability to control her movements. Swimming wasn't like riding a bike. Sometimes you do forget how, especially when the horrifying idea of drowning overtakes your thought process. Her mother was the first to spot her. She yelled for the others on the boat to help and her uncle jumped in and saved her. Her father missed the entire event. He had spent the whole day below deck, too anxiety-stricken to move. Over the years, Hannah had recurring nightmares about her terrifying ordeal. But not last night.

Last night she dreamt that she was floating naked on her back in the middle of an ocean in the dead of night, with no land in sight. The moon was full and round and it lit up the entire sky. The water was devoid of ripples and waves. There was no sound. It was as if the earth's mute button had been pressed. She couldn't even hear herself breathe. For some inexplicable reason, she was without fear. She felt completely at peace. The dream seemed to last the entire night.

In the morning, when she opened her eyes, the first thing she saw was the bedroom ceiling, which was a brownish-yellow color from years of built-up cigarette smoke. She had never noticed it before. She closed her eyes and wished she could fall back to sleep so she could see the moon's magnificent glow again, and return to the peace and tranquility of her dream. But when she opened her eyes, she was faced with the physical reminder of how corroded and discolored her life had become.

Usually the first thing she did in the morning was to smoke at least two or three cigarettes before she even stepped out of bed. But this morning, she got up, went to the bathroom and brushed her teeth. She cupped her hand over her mouth and breathed into it. Her breath smelled clean and fresh. She couldn't wait for Terry and Miranda to notice.

But they were in a rush to get out of the house and never said a word. She just stayed out of their way and they left without even saying goodbye. It was as if they hadn't even noticed her; like she was a ghost. She felt invisible to them.

Yet, despite their treatment of her, she still wasn't tempted to smoke. In fact, what she really wanted was to get some fresh air. It had been three days since she'd even opened a window.

She put on her slippers and slowly unlocked the back door, keeping it open in case she had a panic attack and needed to run back inside. The morning air was still, just like the ocean had been in her dreams. But it wasn't silent. She could hear two squirrels fighting under the porch where she stood. Birds were flying from tree to tree chirping at one another; friendly chirps, not squabbling noises like the squirrels made. Someone was mowing their grass in a nearby yard. She loved the smell of freshly mown grass.

Hannah scanned the backyard until they rested on Miranda's swing set. Thank God it was still there. She could see the seat, beckoning her to come and take a ride. She was determined to overcome her fear and make it to the set. No running back into the house. No failing this time.

She took bold, methodical steps toward the swing, trying to focus on good things like the busy sound of nature, the early morning sun, and the prospect of accomplishing her goal. When she got to the seat, she stopped and looked down at it. Its color had faded from a bright red to a whitish-pink and it was moist with dew. She used the tie of her robe to dry off the seat and then she turned around, grabbed the chains, and began lowering herself down until she felt the seat supporting the weight of her body.

She began to sway back and forth, building momentum with every thrust. Soon she was swinging as high as the swing would let her go.

She couldn't stop smiling. She had finally done it.

She could have swung all day, but her mind was churning with things she suddenly felt like doing. She had been imbued with a newfound energy she hadn't experienced for years, and it was exhilarating. She began to make a mental list of all the errands she planned to run, things she wanted to do, and places she wanted to go.

And one place was at the top of her list.

***

She sat in her car, parked in the garage, staring out the windshield at Terry's sorry excuse for a workbench. She didn't even know why he had one. He never used it. The bright red toolbox appeared as if it'd never been opened.

She wondered if it even contained any tools. *He was not,* she thought, *what you'd call a "handyman."* But she loved him anyway.

She wondered if he still loved her.

Stop it! she told herself. *Stop thinking negative thoughts. Today is going to be a good day. Today is going to be a good day.* She repeated this to herself over and over.

She turned her head and looked down at the rectangular, brown package she had placed on the passenger seat. The sight of it repulsed her. If she didn't get rid of it today, she might never have the nerve or will to do so again. She determined that the post office would be her first errand of the day. Hopefully, the first of many.

Today is going to be a good day...

Chapter Thirty-Six
Maybe His Day Wasn't as Good as Yours

It was still early in the day; Terry couldn't go home. He didn't want to tell Hannah yet that he'd gotten fired. He knew she'd freak out and that was the last thing he needed right now. He would act like it was any other day. He'd pick up Miranda from school and drive her home. He usually went back to the office, but today he'd have to decide on some place to go until he returned home. He had no idea what he was going to do during those hours. He had to figure out an entirely different routine until he was ready to tell Hannah.

As he drove down Merle Haggard Drive, he thought he saw Hannah walking down the street with a package in her hand. He was certain it was her, but by the time he stopped and turned around, she was gone. He was wrong. It wasn't her. Couldn't be her. But if it had been her, that would have been nice.

He smiled at the thought of a Hannah he could run into during the day. He'd honk his horn and she'd turn around with a big, welcoming smile on her face as she ran breathlessly to his car. They'd laugh at the chance of running into each other and decide to make a day of it. Perhaps they'd get a bite to eat or go to the park. Or maybe they'd rent a room in a seedy motel and have wild, unadulterated sex, the kind only cheaters have. But they wouldn't be cheating; they'd only be pretending to be, like they used to do before they had Miranda. And they'd have goofy-ass grins on their faces all evening long as Miranda wondered what was up with her strange, but loving parents. It was a nice thought, but it vanished as quickly as it came.

***

Terry spent most of his day at a used bookstore, although he didn't buy anything. As he left the store empty-handed, the clerk gave him a dirty look and mumbled a curse word under his breath.

He ordered drive-thru at a Mexican restaurant whose name he couldn't pronounce and ate it in the parking lot until it was finally time to pick up Miranda from school.

While he waited in line, he casually looked around for her. She was usually standing apart from the crowd seeking him out with anticipatory eyes. Once she spotted him, she'd wave excitedly and break into a big smile. But he didn't see her. He figured that perhaps she forgot a book and went back into school to retrieve it. She'd probably come running out as soon as his car got to the front of the line.

When he pulled into the front spot and put the car in park, she was nowhere in sight. One of Miranda's teachers—"Mrs. Gray Hair" (he could never remember their names, so he gave them nicknames based on their personal appearance; Miranda especially loved "Mrs. Scowl Face")—approached his car. He lowered the passenger side window and leaned over.

"Mr. Boyle," she said, cheerfully. "What are you doing here?"

"Picking up Miranda," he said. "Like I do every day."

"Oh, I'm sorry," she said, smiling. "Your wife must not have told you. She picked her up already."

"My *wife*?"

"Yeah. She was first in line."

"Did she say where they were going?" he asked, as panic began to set in.

"Home, I assume. Why?"

"But... I pick her up. Every day."

"I know that, but she's on the list. And Miranda confirmed that it was her mother. I'd never met her before. Nice lady."

Terry's stomach twisted and his heart began to race. He had to get home immediately. Something wasn't right. He stepped on the gas, disregarding the school zone speed limit, and pulled out of line. He saw Mrs. Gray Hair in his rearview mirror shaking her finger at him as he sped away. He'd definitely hear it from her tomorrow.

As he tore into his driveway, he noticed Hannah's Prius, which hadn't left the garage in years except for his occasional startups to prevent a dead battery, parked out front.

He jerked to a stop, got out, and ran to the car. He cautiously peered in the window. Empty. Nothing out of the ordinary. He tried the door. It was locked.

He snapped his head to face the house, wondering if Hannah was staring out the window at him like she often did when he returned from work, but there was no one there. He rushed toward the front door, took out his key, and inserted it in the lock—but it was open. Hannah always kept it locked.

The first thing that hit him when he entered the house was the smell—instantly familiar, but startlingly unexpected. And it was coming from their kitchen.

He darted down the hall, bracing himself for what he might discover, but when he got there, it turned out to be nothing he ever could have imagined.

What he smelled was the sweet aroma of home cooking. Hannah's home cooking. The food she used to prepare for him every night before Miranda was born. She was making dinner, and Miranda was sitting at the table quietly doing her homework.

"Hi, Daddy," said Miranda. She looked up at him cheerfully, then went straight back to her homework as if this idyllic tableau of domestic bliss was an ordinary sight in their home.

"How was your day?" chirped Hannah, in an octave she hadn't reached in more than eight years.

"You picked up Miranda from school," he stated dazedly.

"Yeah. Are you proud of me?"

"You scared me half to death. Why didn't you tell me?"

"I wanted to surprise you. I thought you'd be happy. I had a good day today. I finally got out."

He stood there for a moment, completely befuddled. It was too much to process.

"You can go back to work now. Try not to be late tonight. I'm preparing a big dinner."

Terry nodded robotically, turned around, and began to walk down the hall. When he got to the front door, he could hear Miranda and Hannah talking quietly in the kitchen.

"I had a good day today, Miranda," said Hannah.

"I know, Mom. You told me."

"Daddy didn't seem very happy."

"Maybe his day wasn't as good as yours."

Chapter Thirty-Seven
She Couldn't Continue

Terry had a lot of time to think before he returned home from his non-existent job. And he didn't like where his thoughts were taking him.

He should have been so happy that the *old* Hannah was back, even if it proved to be temporary. But it didn't change anything. In fact, it made everything worse. He actually felt anger. He was angry that she expected him to jump up and down with joy just because she had one good day. *One good day.* Did that eviscerate all the misery she'd caused over the past eight years? How could it? All this time he'd held out hope that she would get better and then their life would return to the way it had been, and everything would resume as if those past eight years had never occurred. But that was not the case. It had the complete opposite effect. All the love he once held for her had dissipated. It was buried forever in the memories of their past; captured in a photograph he'd stuffed away on the bottom of a reusable grocery bag.

Today had been pivotal. He no longer had a job and he realized that he no longer loved Hannah. Nothing would ever be the same.

The question now was: *What the hell was he going to do?*

***

Terry leaned in and kissed Miranda on the forehead, and then quickly got up from her bed.

"Aren't you going to read to me tonight?" she asked.

"Not tonight," he said, without turning around. "Tomorrow. I promise."

"How about I read to you then?"

He turned and looked at her. "Sure," he agreed. "You can read to me tomorrow."

"Really? You promise?" she said, smiling in eager anticipation.

"Promise." Just as he was about to turn and leave, he noticed that the vase on her nightstand was empty. "Where are your flowers?" he asked.

"Mommy threw them away."

Terry's blood pressure instantly spiked. "Why would she do that?"

"She said they were dead, but they weren't. They were just thirsty. Will you get me some more?"

"Of course I will," he replied.

She grinned widely as she pulled her covers up to her chin. "Goodnight, Daddy."

"Goodnight, Sweetheart."

When he switched off the lights, they flickered, as they did every night. He reminded himself to call the electrician, as he did every night. But this time he meant it. It was not like he had anything else to do tomorrow.

***

This had always been the most unpleasant part of his day—the long walk from Miranda's bedroom to his own. Tonight it was especially difficult. He dreaded the argument that would invariably transpire once he entered those bedroom doors. As he trudged down the narrow, dimly-lit hallway, he fought to contain the resentment and rage he felt toward the *new* Hannah. He had changed, too.

And he didn't trust what the *new* Terry might say or do, either.

Halfway down the hall, he was blocked by an inconveniently placed wicker clothes hamper. He couldn't help but wonder if Hannah had put it there on purpose to remind him to do the laundry. It wouldn't be the first time she'd done that. He lifted the lid and looked inside. It was empty. This morning it had been overflowing. Hannah had not only cleaned the house, gone grocery shopping, and picked up Miranda from school, but she had done the laundry. He should have been happy.

Instead, he shoved it against the wall, resisting the urge to kick a hole in it.

***

She was sitting up in bed when Terry entered the room. She wasn't smoking and the TV was off.

"I'm actually tired tonight," she said, and then yawned. "A good tired. You know what I mean?"

He mumbled something inaudible and headed straight to the bathroom.

"Where are you going?" she called after him. "I want to talk to you."

He stopped but didn't turn around.

"What?"

"Look at me."

Terry slowly turned to face her. She was wearing a nightgown he'd never seen before.

"What do you want?" he asked coldly.

If she was put off by his detached manner, she wasn't showing it. "For starters, did you like dinner?"

He nodded slightly. "Yes."

"Yes? That's all you've got to say?" She paused, waiting for him to respond. Apparently, it was all he had to say. "I don't think you realize what a big accomplishment it was for me to make dinner. And it was good. Miranda darn near licked her plate. You barely touched yours."

"I wasn't very hungry. Sorry."

"Don't be sorry. It's okay. I forgive you." And then she added, playfully, "But just this once."

He turned away and resumed his walk to the bathroom. Hannah quickly leapt from the bed and cut him off. "I had so much energy today," she said breathlessly. "I got out of the house. Can you believe it?"

All Terry could manage was a fleeting half-smile.

"I ran errands," she continued, "Bought groceries, did the laundry, picked up Miranda." She stopped, but then remembered one more thing. "Oh, and I cleaned the house!"

Terry fixed his eyes on hers. "Yeah, and you threw Miranda's flowers away."

She took a step back as she began to realize the root of his frosty mood. "They were dead."

"No they weren't. They could have lasted a few more days."

"What difference does it make? You can pick her some new ones. They're still in bloom."

"That's not the point. I make the decision when to replace her flowers."

Hannah took a moment to allow his words to register. "So… that's what this is all about. I disrupted your routine. Well, I'm sorry if I got in the way of your *routine*." She elongated *routine* for added emphasis.

Terry began to breathe heavily, trying to control his anger, his temples pounding.

"What is it?" Hannah asked confrontationally. "Are you afraid I'll take away your job as 'Super Dad'? Afraid Miranda will begin to need me more and you less?"

Finally, Terry exploded.

"It was *one* day! You had *one* fucking good day!! How do I know it's going to last? How do *we* know if it's going to last? You've got Miranda's hopes up. I don't want to see her hurt by you anymore. Whatever corner you've taken, whatever obstacle you think you've overcome, you'd better be goddamned sure it's not going to disappear by tomorrow because she won't be able to take it. I won't be able to take it!!"

Hannah collapsed onto the bed and began sobbing. "I'll see a doctor. I'll try to get help. But I can't promise you it's gone for good. I hope to God it is, but I don't know. I just don't know..."

Terry felt like a complete asshole. An unsympathetic, uncaring, unemployed asshole. He wanted to say he was sorry, but he knew that kneejerk apologies were just as harmful as the heated words that preceded them.

"Please go," she said through her tears. "Pick Miranda some more flowers. She'll be so sad if she wakes up tomorrow and..."

She couldn't continue.

Chapter Thirty-Eight
He Would Be So Happy

Hannah listened to his car drive away. Fast. She wondered where he was going. There were plenty of wildflowers within walking distance from their house. She regretted telling him to go, but his words had hurt her deeply. Sometimes he could be so cold and cruel.

He should have apologized, she thought.

Her anxiety began to creep back in for the first time that day. She fought to keep it from escalating, from taking over again. She felt the urge to smoke, but resisted. She wanted to prove him wrong. She was determined to get better. Tomorrow she would make an appointment with a doctor. She would show him that she was trying. She would not fail this time.

She heard footsteps walking down the hallway toward the bedroom door. Her heart began to race with excitement. She was convinced it was Terry. He had parked down the road and ran back to say he was sorry. He was going to tell her that he was proud of her for her accomplishments that day. They would agree not to fight anymore. They would make love instead. It would be the perfect ending to a perfect day.

She stared at the door as it slowly creaked open, barely able to contain the desire to squeal with delight. She drew in a quick breath and held it as the door was pushed all the way open. And then she exhaled loudly.

It was Miranda.

Mother and daughter stared at each other like strangers, struggling to begin a conversation.

"Miranda, what are you doing up?" Hannah finally managed.

"Are you and Daddy going to get a divorce?" Miranda whispered thinly.

Hannah could feel her fear from across the room.

"No, of course not," she said with a forced happy face. "Now go on back to bed."

Miranda stepped into the room. "Where did Daddy go?"

"I... don't know."

"Is he coming back?"

"Of course. Daddy would never leave us," Hannah said, not fully certain if she was being dishonest or optimistic.

Miranda took a tentative step forward.

"Can I wait with you until he comes home?"

Hannah was speechless. Miranda had never asked to do this before and she wasn't prepared with an answer.

Miranda began to walk steadily toward the bed. "I won't take up too much room. I promise."

Hannah's eyes widened as she watched Miranda get closer and closer. Finally, she was standing at the foot of the bed.

"Don't you think you'll be more comfortable in your own bed?" Hannah asked, her voice trembling.

"No. I want to sleep with you."

Hannah's mind was reeling with unease. "I think you..."

"Please, Mommy?" Miranda persisted desperately.

Hannah's shoulders slumped. "I guess it'd be..." Before she could finish her sentence, Miranda leapt onto the bed, slipped under the covers, and wrapped her thin arms around her mother.

Hannah began to shiver with anxiety, her teeth chattering as if she was freezing cold. But Miranda didn't let go. In fact, she held on tighter.

Hannah closed her eyes and tried to suppress the emotion building up inside of her.

"Are you okay, Mommy?"

Hannah nodded rapidly, but was unable to utter a word.

Miranda reached up and began to soothingly stroke Hannah's hair. Her first reaction was to flinch, but Miranda continued, undeterred. Finally she released a slow, controlled breath and began to feel her body relax. Her trembling gradually subsided.

She sat up and enveloped Miranda with her arms, pulling her closer. Mother and daughter sat in the dark, clinging to each other. It was the first time Hannah had held her daughter since she was a baby.

Tears rolled down her face as she imagined Terry's expression when he finally came home and found them cuddling together. He would be so happy.

Chapter Thirty-Nine
I Was Tired of Hearing People Leave

Marv had been counseling Terry for several months. In all that time, he had never talked about "that night."

Marv sat back in his well-worn chair, waiting for Terry to begin speaking, trying not to appear too eager. He knew Terry would eventually come around and open up about it, but he hadn't expected it to happen now. Not this soon. Something major must have occurred to trigger his willingness to talk, but Marv didn't ask him what it was. In fact, he didn't say much of anything. Experience taught him that when a client begins to reveal something they've been suppressing, it was best to just sit back, shut up, and listen.

"I had to get out of there. I drove and drove until I couldn't drive anymore. I never wanted to go back. And I wouldn't have if it hadn't been for..."

Terry stopped midsentence. Marv waited for him to continue, but didn't pressure him. The session had just begun, and they had plenty of time.

Terry remained silent, his eyes squeezed tightly closed. Marv became concerned that he wouldn't continue, so he made the decision to prompt him ever so cautiously. "If it hadn't been for... what?"

Terry took a deep breath, and then continued.

***

Terry had told the story. He had finally gotten it out. Afterward, he was drained, exhausted, but also, surprisingly, relieved. He had the invigorating sensation that his internal maelstrom was slowly starting to subside. That his despair was dissipating. He asked Marv if it was normal to feel this way. Was it too soon? Marv told him that it wasn't about what was normal or too soon. He said that it was about what felt honest. And not to run away from honest feelings, but to embrace them.

Terry released a huge sigh. He was beginning to feel something he hadn't felt since that night—hope. Honest to goodness, hope.

After leaving Marv's office, he pulled over to the side of the road, took out his phone, and dialed her number. "I need to see you. Can you meet me at the hardware store?"

***

W hen Terry drove into the hardware store's parking lot, he spotted Renee sitting on the steps, dangling her cell phone between her legs. She looked pissed off.

"This better be good," she said, as he approached her. "I'm in no mood for games. I made that clear the last time we saw each other. Did you fix your problem? Because it you didn't, you're just wasting my time. And yours."

Terry waited to speak until he reached her. "Did I *fix* my problem? No, I can never fix it. But, I think I'm ready to address it."

"That's... not good enough," she said, and then began to stand up, which prompted Terry to sit down.

"I'm sorry. I didn't ask you to come here so I could tell you what you wanted to hear. I came to tell you what I've been thinking about."

Renee looked at him sideways. "Well, what's that?"

Terry looked up at her and said with all sincerity, "I was thinking that you shouldn't sell this store."

Renee shook her head in displeasure. "Is that what you needed so desperately to tell me? This late at night?"

"It's... *part* of the reason." And then he held out his hand. She saw that he wasn't wearing his wedding ring.

Renee looked at him suspiciously, and then turned away. "You're too late."

Terry sprung to his feet. "What?"

"I said, you're too late. I made my decision already." And then she turned around and looked at him. "I'm keeping the store."

Terry spontaneously threw his arms around her and gave her a hug.

"Whoa. Slow down. What's the matter with you?" she said, pushing him away.

"I'm sorry. I'm just glad to see you."

"See me?" Renee asked.

"Be with you."

Renee took a step back. "Be with me? What does that mean?"

Terry smiled. "What do you think it means?"

"It sounds like you want to have sex with me," Renee said, bluntly.

"No," Terry quickly replied. "Not necessarily. Maybe. Eventually. I... don't know. I haven't thought that far ahead. I just want to take it slow."

"Terry," Renee said, as she put her hands on his shoulders. "You're married."

Terry shook his head, confused.

"I've changed," Renee continued. "I'm not sleeping with married men anymore. I made a vow. Like you did."

"I... don't understand."

"And I finally do. I'm done with men for a while. At least until I figure some things out."

Terry looked at her forlornly. "But, I'm not like those other men."

Renee removed her hands from his shoulders. "You're not? What makes you different?"

"I like you."

This seemed to catch Renee off-guard.

"That's not enough," she said simply, as she began to leave. "Now, if that's all, I'm going to go. I have a big day tomorrow. The painters are coming early and..."

"Wait!" Terry exclaimed, as he followed her.

"Why?"

"Because..." Terry had to think fast. "I want to know more about the changes."

"Changes?" Renee asked.

"Yeah. The changes you're going to make to the store."

Renee paused. "Really?"

"Yes," Terry said, enthusiastically. "I want to know everything. Tell me what you plan to do."

Renee looked at him skeptically for a moment. Then she began to speak. "Well... for starters... the sign. It has to go. I don't care if you like it. It's out of here and there's no changing my mind."

"I understand, if you hate it that much. But I still like it." He went and stood next to her. "So, I have to ask... what made you decide not to sell?"

"It would have been like giving up. And I don't give up."

He nodded his head, smiling. "That's good to know."

They both held their breath, and then released it at the same time. "C'mon. I want to show you something," Renee said, as she bounded up the steps.

She kicked open the inner screen door to the store with the toe of her boot. Terry noticed that the bell didn't ring.

"Did you get rid of the bell?"

"Yup," she said, letting the door slam behind her. "I was tired of hearing people leave."

Chapter Forty
He Was Hiding Something

"What's taking you so long?" Renee called out from down the dark hall. Terry moved quickly toward her voice, wondering what she was in such a hurry to show him. When he reached the office, he looked in and saw her kicking back on a new brown leather sofa. It was a distressed model, designed to look old and worn in, but it was obviously new, due to the strong, pungent odor of fresh pelt that permeated the air. "Well, what do you think?"

"Much better than the old one," he said. "It looks very comfortable. And expensive."

"It was, but it was worth every penny. C'mon," she said, moving over to make room for him. "Sit. Try 'er out."

He strolled over to the sofa with his hands in his pockets and plopped down next to her, their knees barely touching.

"It's nice. And soft," he said as he settled into the cushion.

"Bought this new lamp, too," she said, presenting a stand-alone lamp with an oval shade, dimly lit. "Got it at Home Depot. Gotta check out the competition sometimes."

Terry laughed.

"I have more changes in mind. I was thinking of expanding. Making the store bigger."

He turned to her, close enough to smell her warm, fresh breath.

"Why?"

"What do you mean, why?" she said, looking as if she wasn't expecting him to disagree.

"Because I like it just the way it is. Was," he said, leaning in closer to her. "Look, if I want big and fancy and loud and obnoxious, I'll go to Home Depot. But if I want comfort and charm and great customer service, I'll come here."

She settled back and folded her hands in her lap, looking dejected. "Now you got me all confused."

Terry placed his hands over hers. "I think you shouldn't make too many changes," he said. "That's just my two cents."

***

"Really?" she said, turning to him, zoning in on his soulful, brown eyes—the same eyes she saw in the security mirror the day he entered her life, searching for something he never expected to find.

"Really," he replied, with added emphasis.

For a precarious moment, neither of them moved.

And then Terry leaned in and kissed her gently on the lips. She allowed it—but only for a split second.

"No," she stammered, as she pushed him away. But not too hard.

"No?"

"I've changed. I told you that," Renee said, turning from him.

"So have I," Terry said.

Renee turned back to him. "No, Terry. You really haven't. You're still in the same place you were the day I met you."

Terry jolted upright. "That's not true. You have no idea," he said in a very measured manner.

"What do you mean? No idea about what?" Renee pressed.

"I… can't tell you."

"Why? What is going on with you?"

Terry stared at her for a moment, then stood up. "You're right. Nothing's changed. It'll always be the same. It'll never go away. Never."

Renee got up and went to him. "What won't go away?"

For a moment, he looked like he was going to answer her, then he stopped and began to head for the door. Renee ran to him and cut him off.

"Talk to me."

"I don't want to talk," he said quietly.

Renee leaned in and kissed him. Tenderly. Sweetly. Then she pulled him closer to her and held him. He was shaking. She wanted to comfort him. Who was she kidding? She wanted him. Period. She had tried to change, but she couldn't resist. She had waited too long. It was time.

She pulled away slightly and began to undo the buttons on his shirt. He watched her as she gently undid the first button. And then the second...

***

And then he remembered and jerked away from her. But Renee didn't let go, which caused the shirt to rip open and buttons to spring in every direction.

"NO!" he shouted, as he struggled to cover up.

But it was too late. She had already seen it. And she was shocked.

"Terry... My God... What happened?"

He pushed her aside and staggered haphazardly toward the door of the office. He had to get out of there before she began to ask questions. She'd want to know everything. How? Why? She'd want to know the whole story. The honest truth.

***

Renee made it outside only to see his car tear out of the parking lot.

Yet just in time to memorize his license plate number.

And then he was gone.

Her mind was reeling, wondering what the hell had happened to him. She had to know. She had to find him. She had been right all along.

He *was* hiding something.

Chapter Forty-One
Make Sure and Tell Frank I Said Hello

Connie Marks was working Renee's last nerve.

She'd been standing patiently in front of her desk, staring at Connie's gray roots for almost five minutes without ever being acknowledged. She knew Connie hated her; most women did. But Connie hated her more than most. Because it was personal.

Their relationship dated back to their grammar school days, when they used to be inseparable best friends. When high school came along, so did all the social entrapments that can forever forge or fracture long-term friendships. Some kids will do anything to be popular, and Connie was one of those kids. Renee didn't give a flip. She just wanted to have a good time. And that included sleeping with lots of boys. Most of them had girlfriends, and one of them was Connie's boyfriend. And when Connie found out, she never forgave her.

So, while Renee was quickly branded a *slut*, Connie, a cheerleader, rose to the pinnacle of popularity. Of course, the *popular* girls like Connie could be just as promiscuous as girls like Renee, but their reputations were cloaked in the protective shield of popularity. Sleeping with other popular boys—mostly football players—came with the communal territory and was therefore deemed acceptable, if not downright encouraged, to retain their hierarchal high school social standing.

After repeatedly asking Connie, "Is Gordon in?" Renee finally reached her tipping point. She casually sat down on the corner of the desk and folded her arms, knocking over one of Connie's family photos, which caused a domino effect, tipping over three more. The last one to topple over was a picture of Connie's husband, Frank. This seemed to get her attention.

"Would you mind removing your ass from my desk?" Connie seethed, as she returned the photos back to their upright position.

"Sure thing, Connie. As soon as you answer my question."

Connie perused her desktop calendar and said crisply, "Do you have an appointment with Sheriff Slater?"

"Cut the shit, Connie," she said, standing up and leaning on her desk. "Is he in or not?"

Connie peered at Renee over the top of her drug store cheaters. "What's your order of business?"

"None of your business," Renee said.

"Then I'm afraid he's unavailable." Connie sniffed and went back to clicking at her keyboard.

"Fine, then," said Renee. "I'll handle this myself."

She unsnapped the button of her shirt pocket and pulled out a prehistoric flip phone. She pressed one button and soon they could hear the sound of Gordon's phone ringing through his closed office door. Gordon was on her speed dial for the obvious reason that most of her male "friends" were.

"Hello?" they heard him say after only one ring.

"You busy right now?" she asked, glaring at Connie with a smart-ass grin on her face.

"Not too busy for you," he answered, in a hushed but husky tone that managed to penetrate through his thick, bulletproof office door.

"Then would you please inform your receptionist that I'm here to see you?"

Within seconds, Gordon was standing at his open door, panting like a puppy who'd been waiting eagerly for his owner to return from work.

"I'm an executive secretary." Connie curtly corrected Renee.

"Funny. That's not what I'd call you," said Renee, as she snapped shut her phone, shoved it back in her pocket, and breezed toward Gordon's open door.

"Least I'm not a home wrecker," chided Connie.

"Takes two to tango, Connie. Ever hear that saying?"

Connie scoffed audibly and went back to work.

As Renee was about to enter Gordon's office, she turned around and called out, "Oh, and Connie? Make sure and tell Frank I said hello."

Chapter Forty-Two
Will You Help Me?

Sheriff Gordon Slater was one of those popular football players Renee began fooling around with when she was in high school. Of course, no one knew about it then. He was dating a cheerleader, after all, and Renee was—well, she was not a cheerleader. Not even close. She was known to most of the jocks as "Reliable Renee." And with her spreading reputation, none of the guys could risk dating her publicly.

After high school, when that certain cheerleader went off to college in the big city, she quickly forgot about Gordon. Gordon knew he was never leaving Porterville. He liked his hometown, so he knew he had to find someone from around those parts to marry and settle down with.

But that someone wasn't Renee. It was Connie Marks's best friend, Gloria Spence. But even after they married, it didn't stop Gordon and Renee from hooking up. Not after he had kids, not after Gloria was diagnosed with cancer, not after she went into remission, and not after they celebrated their twentieth wedding anniversary. It stopped the day she slapped Renee in the face in front of Terry at the hardware store.

"I'm so happy to see you," Gordon said, as he swaggered toward her with open arms, a horny look in his eyes.

When he got within arm's distance of her, she put out her arm to stop him, like a traffic cop.

He looked at her, confused. "What's wrong? You never return my calls lately."

"Your wife paid me a visit a while back. Made it real clear where we stood."

"She doesn't call the shots in my life," he objected with his chest puffed out.

"Yes, she does. Trust me. I had a handprint across my face for days to prove she ain't fooling around."

"But we've been doing it for so long. Why stop now?"

"Because I've changed, or at least I'm trying to. Your wife loves you, enough to fight for you. I certainly wouldn't fight for a husband who cheats on me. Don't throw away what you have. Not for someone like me."

His eyes penetrated hers for a moment and then he turned away and strutted back to his desk. "Why did you come here? What do you want? You could have told me this over the phone."

She took a deep breath. "I need your help."

Gordon turned around and looked at her as if he were standing in front of a complete stranger. One he'd just met, and was deeply suspicious of.

"Depends," he said, adjusting his tie. "I've got a very busy schedule."

Renee knew that she was talking to a different man, one who was never a friend. Now she was talking to Sherriff Gordon and she had to choose her words wisely.

"There's someone I need to find."

He looked at her apprehensively. "A man?"

"Yes, a man," she admitted reluctantly. "But it's not what you think." He did not look persuaded, so she continued in earnest, as if arguing a case before an unflappable judge.

"I think there's something seriously wrong with him. And I want to help him."

"Is he married?"

Renee paused. She couldn't lie to him. His life was a lie and she knew you could never lie to a liar. "Yes."

Sherriff Gordon took his time sitting down. "I see. Are you having sex with him?"

"No," she said quickly.

"Do you want to?"

"That's none of your business," she blurted out and then instantly regretted her outburst. "Look, I know it sounds like I'm up to something, but I'm not. I can't go into detail. Please trust me. It's not what you think."

"What's the matter with him?" he asked, as he folded his arms across his chest and sat back in his chair. He seemed to enjoy making her squirm.

"I don't know," she said quietly.

"So, what do you want me to do? Arrest him? Did he break the law?"

"No, I just need to know where he lives. That's all. I know you have the resources." She reached in her back pocket and pulled out a slip of paper. "Here," she said, placing it on his desk. "This is his license plate number."

He looked at the paper, but didn't pick it up.

"Gordon?" she said. "Please?"

He turned away from her. "I don't know if I can help you."

"Can't… or won't?" He still wouldn't look at her. "Please, Gordon? I'm asking as a friend."

"We were never *friends*," he said disdainfully.

"Yeah, I have a lot of those," she said softly. She moved around the desk so he had no choice but to look at her. "So… will you help me?"

Chapter Forty-Three
It Was the First Time They'd Met

Renee had never ridden in her mother's faded green 1995 Oldsmobile Cutlass Ciera. To her, it was an old lady's car, and she wouldn't be caught dead in it.

Tonight, she had no other choice.

Terry's address, which Gordon reluctantly gave her, was located nearly twenty miles out of town and she couldn't very well ride Stud-Muffin there. Not that far, and not this late at night. Since her car had blown an engine over a year ago, she had no other way to get to his house.

The car was still behind the hardware store right where Lois parked it on the day she died. Renee couldn't bring herself to move it. If it hadn't been for the bind she was in, the car most likely would have rusted right there until she decided to call the junkyard to come and haul it away.

She wiped away residue from the window and looked inside. The car keys were dangling from the ignition slot. Lois always left her keys in her car. People in Porterville knew better than to try and steal other people's cars, especially Lois Patrick's car. If anyone was foolish enough to try, she'd have simply removed her pistol from her purse and shot to kill without so much as breaking a sweat.

The moment Renee opened the door, the smell of her mother came wafting out. Like Renee, Lois didn't wear perfume, so it wasn't a store-bought smell. It was a natural combination of bodily scents that were uniquely hers. It wasn't a bad smell, but it was a strong one and it caught

Renee by surprise. She felt her throat tighten and found herself struggling to fight back tears. She hadn't anticipated having such an overwhelming, visceral reaction. She thought she was through with the mourning and the tears, but obviously she wasn't.

As soon as she got in the car, she rolled down the window. She could dilute the smell of her mother, but she couldn't avert her eyes from the countless visual reminders she was surrounded by. The purple, knitted piece of yarn she used as a key chain. The tissue crammed into the crevice of the seat. The rosary hanging from the rearview mirror. The coffee-stained Starbucks cup. *Starbucks?*

Since when did Lois start going to fucking Starbucks?!

And then Renee remembered that there were many things she never knew about her mother.

She closed her eyes tightly and started the car. As the engine turned over, the radio blasted a conservative talk show station at full volume. Renee quickly switched the station off, and put the car in drive.

She drove in silence, thinking about what the hell she was going to do once she got to Terry's house.

***

After locating the address on a black iron mailbox situated at the end of a driveway so long that the house couldn't be seen from the road, Renee backed up and parked the car a safe distance from the entrance. She got out of the car and began maneuvering through the dense forest of trees, far enough away not to be seen, but close enough to keep the twists and turns of the winding driveway in her sight. This was the type of forest you wouldn't want to get lost in.

The driveway must have been a mile long. At least that's how it felt to her. When she finally spotted the house through the thick trees, she stopped dead. This couldn't be where Terry lived. She began to wonder if Gordon was tricking her to get her back for ending their affair.

First of all, the house, if you could call it that, didn't even look habitable. It looked like a cinder block fortress. Or a bunker. Who would raise their family in such a place? She had envisioned him living in some place a boring insurance salesman with a spotless Volvo would own. Some place more conventional. More suburban-looking. More normal.

Then it hit her. Did she even know who he was? They'd spent very little time together. Yes, they had a strong and instant connection from the very first moment they met. At least she thought they did. Maybe it was just her. Maybe he didn't feel the same way. Maybe he was just being nice. She was beginning to think that their entire relationship was all created in her mind and she didn't know who he was at all. Everything he told her could be nothing but lies. He could be a serial killer, for all she knew. Did his family even exist? She couldn't be certain of anything. All she knew is that she had fallen in love with him. Whoever he was.

She stood in the dead of night, hoping to see some sign of life inside the house. All she could see was one interior light, most likely coming from the kitchen, due to the brightness it cast out into the nighttime air. She wanted to see more, but she couldn't risk turning on her flashlight for fear of being spotted. That had happened too many times in the past, and it was never a happy surprise. She quickly learned how expendable she was to men who had affairs. Once you got too close to their lie they called a life, it was over—they had all seen *Fatal Attraction*.

She heard a strange clicking noise behind her and snapped her head around to see what it was. It was too dark to identify, but she convinced herself it was some sort of harmless animal. Or at least she hoped it was. She began to become increasingly uneasy being surrounded by all the ominous looking trees, clustered together so closely that they obscured the sky and prohibited an easy access out. And the strange noises all around her didn't help, either. She kicked herself for not bringing her gun. She had forgotten her mother's advice:

"Always carry your gun on you. You never know when you may need it."

She became fixated on the house. Something about it didn't seem right, but she couldn't put her finger on it. Something Terry said at some point led her to believe he lived in a house much different than this one. Why was the picture she had created in her mind nothing like what she was looking at? She replayed all the conversations she'd had with him in her head, but couldn't think of anything in particular. He didn't talk much about where he lived, but on the few occasions he had, she'd taken special notice. She liked getting a glimpse into his world. She reveled in the details. The details…

And then she remembered.

It was the first time they'd met.

Chapter Forty-Four
And He Was Gone

Renee whipped out her phone and stabbed the speed dial button designated for Gordon's number with her middle finger. She was so pissed off she could hardly catch her breath. How could he do this to her? Was he that immature? She waited impatiently as the phone rang endlessly, trying to contain her anger.

The call went straight through to voicemail. It was his wife's recorded voice cheerfully asking the caller to "please leave a message and Sheriff Gordon will return your call as soon as he has the chance."

She waited for the three beeps and after the final prolonged *b-e-e-e-p*, she tore into him.

"How could you do this to me, Gordon? This is not Terry's house. The first time he came into the store he bought fire escape ladders. Why would he need them for a one-story house? You knew that and sent me on this wild goose chase on purpose. I'll bet you think you're really funny. Well, I think you're just mean. And a prick." And then she added, "And a terrible lay," before she snapped the phone shut and shoved it back in her pocket.

She was torn about what to do next. She could just leave and forget about the whole thing. But on the other hand, she had come this far, so there was no harm in going a little further now that her curiosity was piqued. She desperately wanted to see who lived in that house. Who would live in a bunker tucked so far away in the middle of a dense forest? It could be anyone or no one at all. Either way, she was determined not to leave until she found out. Even if it meant, quite possibly, risking her life.

Put one foot in front of the other, she repeated to herself, trying to build up the courage to approach the house. Finally, she willed her body forward, trying to make as little noise as humanly possible. Unfortunately, her cowboy boots made that task simply unfeasible. You can't tiptoe in shit-kickers. And you can't walk quietly. But it wasn't like she had a choice; they were the only kind of shoes she owned. She winced every time she set down her foot, as she inevitably landed on something that either snapped, popped, squished, or squirmed away.

As she got closer, she could see through the window with the interior light on. There were no curtains, so she had an unobstructed view, and the first thing that caught her attention was a faucet spout. It was a kitchen, all right. There was a white, ancient refrigerator with curved edges similar to the kind she'd seen on reruns of *I Love Lucy*. There was something stuck to it with a magnet, but she couldn't make out what it was from where she was standing. Next to the refrigerator was a small vintage stove with two burners. She noticed that one of the cupboard doors was open, but she couldn't see what was in it. She had to get closer.

Just as she was about to move forward, she saw him enter the room. His back was turned to her but that didn't matter.

It was Terry.

She'd recognize that back, that walk, from a mile away.

She quickly hid behind a tree so he wouldn't see her when he turned around. By the time she glanced back around the trunk, the cupboard door was shut.

And he was gone.

Chapter Forty-Five
He Looked Confused, Angry, and a Little Scary

Renee couldn't risk Terry or his family seeing her, so she had no choice but to do it the hard way—by getting down on her hands and knees and crawling toward the kitchen window. Part of her said she was too old for this nonsense, and the other part said to press on. The press on part won out.

When she finally reached the house, she leaned against the wall and tried to catch her breath. Her heart was pumping so loudly she thought the sound would reverberate through the walls. Thank God they were built out of cinder block.

Doubt began to creep in again. What if he returned to the room and caught her? What if Hannah and Miranda were sitting at the table and saw her? How would she explain herself? She was so close. Too close to turn back. She said a short prayer and then crept up until she barely cleared the edge of the kitchen windowsill. And then she looked inside.

The kitchen was empty. And sparse and cold and white and very clean. She scanned the room until she had the refrigerator in sight. She could now identify what was attached to it. It was a brightly colored collage consisting of ripped up pieces of construction paper that depicted a field of California wildflowers—obviously one of Miranda's school art projects. It was impressive for such a young girl. Renee wondered if Hannah helped her. Crazy people tended to be quite artistic.

Just then, Terry came back in the room.

She quickly dropped down, hoping he hadn't seen her. She struggled to control her racing heart by taking slow, deep, labored breaths. She rested her back against the wall and closed her eyes. *Relax*, she told herself. She was safe. He hadn't seen her. But then she heard footsteps approaching. Light footsteps. Like someone was sneaking up on her. A child's footsteps? She was afraid to look, but as the footsteps got closer, she knew she had to see who or what it was. So she slowly opened her eyes.

It was a fawn. Renee released a sigh of relief. It hadn't even noticed her. She watched it as it casually walked on by, no clue that it had nearly given her a fatal heart attack.

She leaned her head back against the wall and looked upward. She could see the ceiling of the kitchen. Her jaw dropped. She had to blink twice to make sure her mind wasn't playing tricks on her.

The entire ceiling was covered in smoke detectors, spaced about a foot apart.

What the hell was going on? she thought. *Why would Terry need so many smoke detectors? You'd have to be crazy to install that many when just one would do the trick.*

But then she remembered Hannah, and how Terry had described her predilection for needing to feel *safe*. Her initial reaction had been right: Hannah was crazy.

She had to decide what to do next. Obviously Terry hadn't seen her, or he'd have certainly come outside and busted her by now. But she couldn't risk looking in the window again. She knew she might not be so lucky the next time.

She turned her head to the side and noticed a small ray of light coming from the other side of the house. Unlike the harsh kitchen light, this one was softer, warmer—the type of light that a small lamp might project. She crept around the side of the house, moving toward the light until she was directly under the window. She could see sheer Hello Kitty curtains loosely suspended from a simple aluminum rod inside the frame of the window. This had to be Miranda's bedroom. Thankfully, the curtains were thin enough to allow her to see through them without being seen. She slowly stood up, looked inside the room, and almost had to shield her eyes from the blinding bright pink walls. Renee hated the color pink. It was too "girly-girl." She couldn't even recall the color of her room as a young girl. All she remembered were the posters of horses. And her father coming in at night.

On the nightstand beside the bed was a glass vase of fresh pink Cosmos. Miranda's bed was empty and still made up. Renee looked at her watch. Ten o'clock and she still wasn't in bed. And then she remembered that it was Friday. Perhaps she was allowed to stay up late on the weekends.

She looked up at the ceiling. More smoke detectors. The ceiling was covered with them. What were they doing to this young girl? She should be staring up at cloud murals, not smoke detectors. She had to stop looking at the room. It was too depressing.

She decided to return to the kitchen window for another look. She crouched down as low as she could and made her way toward the light. Just then, she tripped over something round and tubular that made a loud, clanging noise whose echo seemed to linger on forever. Renee fell backwards, landing squarely on her ass. It hurt like hell, but she couldn't dwell on the pain. All she could think about was how, at that very moment, the jig was up. Surely they heard the noise and would come running outside any second to see what it was. Renee lay there in the dark, waiting to hear a door open or a voice call out, but it was completely silent.

She craned her neck to see what she had tripped over. She couldn't see it at first. It appeared to be a pile of cylinder tubes. They were too thin to be pipes. And then she saw two chains wrapped around a child's swing and realized that it was the pieces to a swing set. They had been stacked in a pile next to the house.

She sat up and winced in pain. She was certain that tomorrow she'd have a huge bruise on her butt, along with a splitting headache. She began to wonder if all of this was worth it. And then she remembered what she had seen when she ripped off Terry's shirt. And she knew she couldn't leave until she got some answers.

She brushed a few dried leaves from her hair, wiped the cold dirt from her seat, and began to creep toward the window again. Even though she was in pain, she had a newfound burst of energy. She wasn't leaving until she got one more look. She finally reached the window, and after taking a few quick, catch-up breaths, she cautiously looked in again.

Terry was sitting at the kitchen table with his back to her, and he was completely motionless. She could see the corner of a white cardboard box on the table in front of him, but his body obscured her line of vision so she couldn't be sure what it was.

Just as she was about to move a bit to the right to get a better look, her phone rang. *Loudly.* Her ring tone was Toby Keith's song *A Little Less Talk and A Lot More Action* set at full volume. She loved that song, but *not now!* It was Gordon calling back. She just knew it. He was screwing with her even when he wasn't aware of it.

Damn him!

Panicked, she fumbled in her pocket for her phone and managed to shut it off.

When she looked back up, Terry was staring at her through the kitchen window. He looked confused, angry, and a little scary.

Chapter Forty-Six
Dead

Terry was not happy to see her; she could gauge that by his steely, penetrating gaze. She had infiltrated his sacred place, his home. She had soiled it with her presence. At best, she was a pathetic stalker, and at worst, an unwelcome intruder. He could shoot her for trespassing if he wanted to, and he'd be in the right. She didn't know what he was going to do, or say, so she sweated it out like a convicted felon about to hear her sentence.

He finally spoke, his voice muffled and barely audible through the kitchen window.

"Go away," he said firmly.

"No."

He narrowed his eyes. "Please."

"No. I'm not leaving," she said determinedly, summoning up a courage that surprised even her. "If you want to call the cops, you can use my phone. I have most of their numbers on speed dial."

He began to back away from the window, his eyes still locked on hers. She knew he probably hated her now, but she wasn't about to relent.

"Are Hannah and Miranda home?" she asked.

"I want you to go," he said in an insistent tone.

"No," she persisted. "Do you want to come outside?"

He looked at her incredulously. *"No."*

"Do you want me to come inside?"

He dropped his head and shook it from side to side in disbelief. She knew that he knew she wasn't going anywhere.

He raised his head and looked at her dispassionately, and then turned and walked out of the room.

Renee moved around the house toward the direction he had headed. And then she heard a *click*. It sounded like someone was unlocking the front door.

***

Renee stood in front of the door, her arms folded tightly across her chest to steady her nerves. She could hear a myriad of clanking noises coming from inside—bolts sliding, chains rattling, keys twisting.

Why did he need such excessive protection? she wondered.

He lived in a cement structure in the middle of the woods for God's sake, not in some dingy apartment in a crime-ridden area of New York City. Finally, the clanging ceased, and she heard footsteps receding away from the door.

When the sound of the footsteps subsided, she reached out tentatively and tried the knob. It was open. She turned it to the right, pushed open the door ever so slightly, and stuck her head inside.

"Terry?" she called out. Her voice echoed—*Terry?*

There was no response.

She found it peculiar that the house had no smell. Every family has their unique *smell*. Rarely can one smell one's own, but others can, especially when they first enter a home. After awhile the intensity diminishes, though it never goes away. But Renee smelled nothing. Not perfume, not scented candles, not even the after-odor of a home-cooked meal. The only thing she smelled was the absence of life.

There was a light at the end of the hall. She closed the door quietly behind her and began walking toward it. The hallway was narrow and dark and not one picture adorned the walls. All the doors to the rooms were shut. There was a pink glow radiating from the bottom of one of them. Miranda's room.

When she reached the archway of the kitchen door, she saw Terry sitting at the table, his head in his hands. She stayed in the doorway and waited for him to look up.

After a few moments she said, softly, "Terry? Are you okay?"

"Why did you come here?" he said through his hands.

"You ran away. I had to find you."

"You shouldn't have."

"What's going on? Where's Miranda? Your wife?"

She waited for a response, but didn't receive one. Again— "Terry?"

"Gone," he said stoically.

"What?"

"I said… they're gone."

"Gone? Gone where?"

He began to rock slowly back and forth.

"Did she leave you? Did she take Miranda? Where are they, Terry?"

Slowly, he removed his hands from his face and looked up at her with a haunted, vacant look in his eyes.

"Dead."

Chapter Forty-Seven
And Then He Began to Tell the Story

"*D*ead?"

The word struck Renee like a brutal blow to the gut. For the first time in her life she felt like she was going to faint. She reached out for the closest wall so she wouldn't collapse on the black and white linoleum flooring that kept coming in and out of focus.

She could barely speak. "I... don't understand. When?"

"Three hundred and sixty three days ago."

She tried to get her mind around the significance of the precise number he uttered, without taking even a moment to calculate it. Three hundred and sixty three days. Two days less than a year.

"So they were dead this whole time? Ever since we met?"

He slowly nodded his head. "Yes."

Memories flooded her mind. Suddenly everything made sense, while simultaneously making no sense whatsoever. She tried to grasp the fact that Hannah and Miranda were dead before Terry ever stepped into her hardware store. How could that be? How could she not have picked up on it?

Thinking back, there were clues. His discomfort talking about them—even mentioning their names. His perpetual ghostlike gaze, as if his mind was stuck on a disturbing image or a thought he couldn't quite shake. His tendency to flee whenever Renee pushed him too far intimately. The way he trembled at times for no apparent reason. His habit of twisting his ring around his finger. And a conversation they had that had never sat right with her:

"I told you I don't hate my wife! I loved her!"

"Loved her? So you don't love her anymore?"

"That's not what I meant. I meant to say that I love her."

"How?" she asked delicately, desperate to know more.

"No," he said.

"You have to tell me," she said.

"No."

"Yes."

"It hurts too much."

"It'll make you feel better if you talk to someone."

"I talk to my shrink. He helps," he said. "Helped the other day. The day I called you to meet me at the store. That was the best day I'd had for a long time. And then... I couldn't."

"Couldn't what, Terry?" she gently urged.

"Explain. Not then. I wasn't ready. I just wanted to see you. I finally felt good for the first time since..."

"Since?" she asked.

"Since it happened."

Renee felt stable enough to walk now, so she went over to the table and sat on a chair across from Terry. "I want to know what happened," she said. "I'm your friend. I want to help."

"I don't need your help. And you're not my friend. You're..." he said, trailing off.

"I'm what?"

"I don't know," he said.

"I'm someone who cares about you and I think that makes me a friend."

"You don't even know me," he said.

"I know enough, but not nearly as much as I should. Or would like to."

He stared at her with a remote look in his eyes. "You can go now."

"I know I can," she said. "But I'm not going to. So we can just sit here all night, or you can begin to talk."

He remained silent.

"Okay," she said. "I get it. You don't want to talk. Or maybe you don't know where to begin. Well, let me ask you some questions then. Just tell me when you want me to shut the hell up. I probably won't, but there's no harm in asking anyway."

He still didn't respond.

"How did they die?" she began slowly.

He shook his head from side to side and then got up and walked over to the window and stared into the blackness of the night.

She waited for him to say something, but he just stood there stiffly; a mere shadow of a man.

Renee looked at the white, rectangular box in the center of the table. She glanced up at Terry. He was still looking out the window, his back turned to her. She slowly reached out and lifted the lid slightly so she could get a glimpse inside.

Her heart sank.

It was a pink birthday cake with a floral design outlining the edges. In the center, the letter "M" was written in professional and precise cursive.

She looked up and noticed that Terry had turned back around. He was breathing heavily, painfully. With his gaze fixated on the box he said quietly, "She would have been nine today."

He sighed and launched into his story...

Chapter Forty-Eight
She Would Be So Happy

"It was two days after her eighth birthday. I had gotten fired from my job that morning and didn't know how to tell Hannah. I knew the news would push her over the edge and I wasn't prepared to deal with that.

"When I went to pick up Miranda from school, I found out that Hannah had already been there. I was shocked. I didn't know why she would pick her up. What was she planning to do? Did she kidnap her? Hurt her? Or something worse.

"I rushed home to find something I hadn't been expecting—not even in my wildest dreams. Hannah was making dinner and Miranda was doing her homework, just as normal as can be. They both acted as if this was something that occurred every day. Hannah seemed happier than I'd seen her in ages, almost back to normal. And Miranda looked so content and cheerful. Like her dream had come true.

"I... didn't know how I felt about it. It made me suspicious, uneasy, distrustful, and angry. For eight years, we all lived as captives to her mental condition and that day she shrugged it off, as if life could just go on as if nothing had ever happened. It made me wonder if she'd been faking it all those years. It seemed so... selfish. How could she undergo such a drastic change in one day? What had triggered it?

"And then it hit me. I had been waiting and hoping for eight long years for my life—*our* lives—to return to normal. And on that day, it was normal. But it didn't matter anymore. I had been in love with the idea that one day there would be a normal Hannah again. But it wasn't a normal Hannah I yearned for. It was the old Hannah. And she could never be that. She had changed and I had changed. It was over. My feelings for her were gone. And they would never come back.

"How was I going to tell her that I no longer loved her? Not only did I not love her, I resented her. I could barely even look at her. I had to get out of there. I had to think about what I was going to do.

"So, after I put Miranda to bed, I left.

"I just drove and drove. I didn't know where I was going. I just had to get away. I thought about never going back. And I wouldn't have, if it hadn't been for..."

***

Terry's foot pressed on the gas pedal, causing the speedometer to slowly creep up to eighty miles per hour. Soon it blew past ninety, then ninety-five. He had no idea how fast he was traveling, nor did he care. He just needed to feel speed. And distance.

His hands gripped the steering wheel so tightly that the bones beneath his knuckles looked as though they might bust through his skin. Sweat poured down his face, dripped into his eyes, and obscured his vision. Everything that had been building up in him for the past eight years had finally reached the boiling point. He couldn't contain it any longer. He had lost all sense of control. His thoughts were jumbled and incoherent.

What the hell was he going to do now?

He started to entertain the unthinkable as he watched the road in front of him whiz beneath the car.

It would be so easy, he thought.

Just a quick jerk on the steering wheel and it'd all be over. All of his problems would be gone. No more stress. No more worries. No more . . .

But then something caught his eye.

It was Miranda's artwork lying on top of the bag of personal belongings he had packed from his office. The only thing he truly cared to take with him.

Miranda. What about Miranda? What would happen to her life if he took his? Suicide was no longer an option. Saving her was.

He pulled the car to the side of the road and shut the engine off. He needed a moment to collect his thoughts, to slow down his racing mind. He reclined his seat, leaned back on the headrest and closed his eyes. Memories of Miranda infiltrated his mind. The day she was born (the same day Hannah changed). Her first word ("Dada"). Her first step (on her first birthday). Her first birthday (a Hello Kitty theme). Her triumph on the swing set (after two months of trying). The books he read to her and the way she clung to every word he said (their nighttime ritual). Her desire to show him how well she could read (which he repeatedly resisted). The look on her face when he finally relented and said she could read to him tomorrow night. (*Tomorrow night!*) He had promised her that there would be a tomorrow night.

His thoughts shifted to Hannah. The day they met. Their first date. Their first kiss. The first time they made love. Their wedding. Their honeymoon. Their first years together. Their years before Miranda. Their years after Miranda. And today. *Today!* She had a good day today and he was so self absorbed, so consumed with his own problems, that he couldn't be happy for her. He picked a fight. He said cruel, awful things. He never apologized. He felt bad about that. He *did* care. He didn't know if he loved her, but he *cared*. That was enough for now. He had been there through the good times and the bad. The bad could be behind them. There could be good times ahead. She could get better. She was willing to try. He realized that he was willing to try, too. And hopefully, someday, he might even fall in love with her again.

Terry was exhausted. His mind needed a respite from all the turbulent activity occurring in his brain. He was so tired he could barely keep his eyes open. He tried to stay awake, but couldn't resist.

Just a few minutes, he told himself, *and then I'll go back home.*

And then he fell asleep.

***

"*Daddy!*"

He awoke with a start, convinced that Miranda had called out to him. He looked at his watch: 12:56 in the morning. He turned his head around to the back seat, expecting to see her there, but all he saw was her empty car seat. He was completely disoriented and had to remind himself where he was and how he'd gotten there.

He shut his eyes and rubbed them vigorously. He was wide awake now. And ready to go home.

As he reached for the key in the ignition he remembered the wildflowers. Miranda would expect to see a full bouquet on her nightstand when she woke up. He wasn't going to disappoint her. He got out of his car and went about the task of picking just the right ones to fulfill a promise he made to her and vowed he'd never break.

After he was done picking a bouquet for Miranda, he decided to pick one for Hannah.

Tears rolled down his face as he imagined her expression when he presented them to her. She would be so happy.

Chapter Forty-Nine
And Then He Passed Out

The first thing he saw was thick black smoke as it drifted upwards, obliterating the stars and the moon in the nighttime sky.

Terry stopped his car and looked through his windshield at a scene his mind could not fathom. There was a smattering of firemen in yellow jumpsuits and bright red fire trucks and flashing lights and overlapping hoses and gushing water and people standing around looking helpless and horrified.

He heard shouting, crackling noises, people crying, glass shattering, and sirens wailing.

He was sure he was dreaming. This couldn't be happening. This couldn't be his house.

He shut his eyes. When he opened them again he could still see the thick black smoke, the firemen, the fire trucks, the flashing lights, the hoses, the gushing water, and the people standing around.

He realized it wasn't a dream. This was really happening. His house was on fire.

And Miranda and Hannah were inside.

He bolted out of his car and sprinted toward the house, his feet barely making contact with the ground. Blurred faces turned and stared at him. Neighbors. Strangers. They began to recognize him. Hands tried to hold him back.

That's him! Somebody stop him!

Nothing could stop him. He had to get inside and save his family.

As he entered the house, snake-like smoke coiled menacingly around his feet. Unbearable heat engulfed him, instantly singeing all the hair on his body. He held his mouth shut tightly while he raced down the hallway towards the kitchen. The floor beneath him was littered with sharp objects and smoldering debris that crunched beneath his feet, some of it cutting through his shoes. A light fixture burst over his head, sending fragments of hot glass shooting everywhere. Jagged fragments punctured his bare back, but he didn't feel it. All of his senses were focused on finding Hannah and Miranda.

When he reached the kitchen, he saw a flurry of flames pierce through the dark haze and cast flashes of light on the results of their fierce destructive powers. Burnt, blackened curtains framed the blown-out kitchen window. Paint on the walls curled and crept downwards toward the buckled-up floor. Plastic bowls, stacked up in the sink, were melted almost beyond recognition.

Terry ducked his head down to avoid a dangling beam and headed toward the scorched stairway, wheezing heavily. Rushing up, his foot busted through one of the brittle steps. As he jerked it free, the serrated edges of the wood ripped a gash in his ankle. He continued to limp up the stairs, two at a time. Finally, he reached the top and headed toward Miranda's room.

The door was open. He ran in and did a frantic scan around the room. Miranda's pink walls were soiled with gray soot. The empty vase on her nightstand had shattered. Her collection of dolls was melted together, their faces incinerated by the intense heat. He stepped on one of Miranda's flip-flops and it stuck to the bottom of his shoe like a piece of chewed gum. She wasn't in her bed or under it. He checked the closets and behind the doors; all empty.

He ran down the hallway, stepping on pieces of shattered glass and splintered flooring, while he made his way to the door of his bedroom. He passed a pile of ashes that used to be the wicker clothes basket.

The bedroom door had been kicked in and the red hot hinges hung twisted and contorted on what remained of the door frame. Nothing was left of the bed but a pile of smoldering ashes. He searched the room frantically. No one was in the closet, the bathroom, the shower. No one was anywhere in the room. It was empty.

They had both escaped.

Just then, the floor of the attic above him caved in, triggering an avalanche of melted plastic boxes packed with Christmas decorations to rain down on top of him, knocking him to the ground. As he struggled to get up, one of the hot, smoldering boxes soldered itself onto the flesh on his chest.

And then he passed out.

Chapter Fifty
It Tasted Sweet

"They never got out. The firefighters found them holding each other in our bed. The coroner couldn't pinpoint the exact time of death, but I knew it. She cried out to me in my dream that night. *'Daddy!'* It was 12:56 in the morning."

He took a moment before he continued.

"My first thought was that it was her fault—that she had fallen asleep with a cigarette and..." He couldn't finish the sentence.

"But they later they told me it was faulty wiring. There was a short in an outlet in the upstairs hallway. I never even knew we had an outlet there. It was hidden behind a wicker clothes basket."

He stopped talking.

***

Renee sat at the table with her head down. Tears flowed from her eyes, spilling onto her lap.

She thought about the first time he walked into her store. He was a man with a broken heart and a broken mind. He hadn't let himself believe it and he was living as if nothing had happened. His mind wouldn't allow him to go there. He believed that there was something he could do to make them come back, to somehow change the past—a past so devastating that he had retreated from the world.

Until the day he walked into the hardware store and met her.

She lifted her head and wiped the tears from her face with the back of her hand. "And you? How did you get out?"

"The firemen found me."

Terry walked mechanically over to the cupboard to get a drinking glass. When he opened the door, Renee saw that it was jam-packed with safety supplies—flashlights, duct tape, canned goods, fire extinguishers, earthquake kits, fire escape ladders…

He returned to the sink, poured himself a glass of water, and took a long drink. When he finished, he filled up the glass and drank it down again.

Renee cleared her throat. She got up and walked over to him.

"Turn around," she said, as she gently placed her hands on his shoulders. "I want to see."

He turned around and faced her, confused about what she meant. She slowly began to undo the buttons on his shirt. His eyes followed her actions, letting his arms hang submissively by his sides. When his shirt was fully unbuttoned, she opened it and stood back. His entire chest and torso were covered with extensive, protruding skin grafts.

"Does it hurt?" she asked.

"No," he said. "I'm… numb."

She gently traced her finger along the markings.

"You were shocked," he said, as he gazed down at her hands moving over the terrain of his scars.

"I wouldn't say shocked," she said, transfixed. "More like surprised. I wasn't expecting it. It doesn't bother me, though. Not in the least." She looked up at him and smiled. "You should see my cellulite. Now that's a sight that'll shock you."

The corner of his mouth lifted slightly. It wasn't a full smile, but it was a start. She tenderly took his hands in hers. "What are you doing?"

He furrowed his brow. "What do you mean?"

She stared up at the multitude of smoke detectors covering the ceiling. "What's all that for?"

He followed her eyes to the ceiling. "We should have had more smoke detectors..."

Renee went to the cupboard where he had gotten the drinking glass, and opened it. "And this?"

"She wanted me to install safety equipment and stock up on supplies just in case something terrible happened. There was so much more I could have done to protect them. To make them safe. But I never did. I was too preoccupied. Too busy. She tried to warn me time and time again and I just thought she was crazy."

"She *was* crazy! She was terrified of life. You can't live that way. You can't shield yourself off from the world. You can't prevent all the crap that can happen to you. It's impossible. It wasn't your fault."

"Of course it was."

She grabbed his shoulders firmly, forcing him to look at her.

"No, it wasn't! It was a terrible accident. You can't blame yourself. It'll drive you crazy." She looked up at the smoke detectors and added, "*More* crazy. You gotta knock that shit off. It's not going to bring them back."

"I can't let go," he said, breaking free from her grip.

"You have to. You have to go on with your life. We all have terrible, horrible things in our past that we've got to let go of. I've had to."

He looked at her, offended by what she'd just said. "Nothing compared to what happened to me."

"I wasn't comparing, you shit!" she said. "I was relating!"

"You don't understand!" he yelled out. "You can't relate! No one can!"

She took a deep breath before continuing. "I'm sorry. You're right. I have no idea what you went through."

He leaned against the wall and slid down to the floor. "I'll never get over it. Never."

"No, you won't," she said as she moved to him. "I'm sorry. It's the truth. But time... it helps."

Renee crouched down and sat next to him on the floor. She placed her arm around his shoulders and pulled him close.

He collapsed into her arms and wept softly.

The room was silent except for the steady low rumble emanating from the refrigerator and the faint beating of his broken heart.

They remained on the floor, holding each other until the sun's early rays streamed through the kitchen window. Neither of them had spoken a word all night. Renee was the first to break the silence.

"I don't know about you, but my ass is killing me."

Terry stifled a laugh.

"You can laugh once in a while, you know," she said. "It's the only way you're going to get through this life."

Renee took his hand and led him over to a chair. And then she stepped back away from the table.

"I'm going to go now. But before I do, I want you to know something. You said you like me. Well, I like you, too. A lot. In fact, I think I love you. I don't know how you feel about me. But, if you want to start something, like a relationship... I'm available. I think we can help each other. Think about it. Take your time. And when, and if, you're ready, you know where to find me."

And without saying another word, she left.

***

He watched as she walked away, allowing her words to resonate in his mind. And in his heart.

After he heard the door close, he turned and saw the white box that contained Miranda's birthday cake. He reached over, pulled it toward him, and lifted the lid.

It was a beautiful cake. She would have loved it.

He dipped his finger into the frosting. Then he brought it up to his mouth and licked it.

It tasted sweet.

Epilogue

The day he was released from the burn center in Bakersfield, Terry moved away, returning only for brief check-ups to ensure that the graft had taken, and that he was free from infection. He knew he would never live there again. He couldn't deal with people staring at him, feeling sorry for him, wondering how he was coping, and asking painful questions. He didn't tell anyone where he was going. He just wanted to get away to a place where no one could find him.

Today he made the decision to return. There was someone he needed to see at the post office.

***

Like most of Bakersfield, Giles Kreely was devastated to hear what happened to Terry and his family. He knew more about Terry than most people did. Giles worked at the post office and was extremely gregarious. He loved children, especially Miranda. He and his wife couldn't have kids so they treated all the children of the community as their own.

After he heard about the fire, Giles stopped by the hospital to see Terry, but Terry refused to see him. He didn't want any visitors. Giles understood, so he left without question. But he wrote Terry a note and asked one of the nurses to give it to him.

Terry: I'm so sorry about what happened. I know you are in a lot of pain. If you ever need anything, I am here for you. I am holding your mail at the post office. I had nowhere to deliver it to so I'll hold it for you until you're ready to pick it up. There's a lot waiting for you. Tons of cards. You might want to read them. Might make you feel a little better. People are real sad for you. My wife cries every night. Can't say I haven't done the same. Your friend, Giles. P.S. When you come by, I have something I want to tell you. Something I think you should know.

***

Terry got the note, but didn't respond. He didn't want to read the cards. There was nothing anyone could say that would change what happened or make him feel better. But he was always curious about what Giles wanted to tell him.

He was ready to hear it now.

He stood in line and waited patiently behind the only other customer in the post office—a stocky woman with a pronounced slouch and a tightly coiled perm. Terry could hear the conversation she was having with Giles. She was sending a care package to her son overseas. Giles asked how her son was doing and the woman said he was doing as well as could be expected. This was his third deployment, after all. Then Giles asked her how *she* was doing and she said that it was tough on her and it never got easier. In fact, it got harder every day.

Time doesn't heal all wounds, Terry thought to himself.

The woman kissed the package and slid it across the counter to Giles. She nodded her head, and left quickly. She looked like she was trying to wait until she was safely in her car before breaking down in tears.

Giles carefully placed the package in a canvas bin before he looked up and began saying what he said to every customer: "Can I help..." He stopped mid-sentence when he saw Terry standing in front of him. For a moment he was speechless. But, just for a moment.

"Terry!" Giles exclaimed. "It's so good to see you again. I was hoping you'd come back. Gosh, I tell ya, it's really, really good to see you. What are you up to? Where you been? I was—"

"I can't stay," Terry interrupted before Giles could ramble on any further.

"Oh," Giles said.

"You left me a note when I was recovering in the hospital," Terry said, getting right to the point. "Said you have some mail for me."

"Yeah. We knew you wouldn't be going home—" Giles stopped himself and then corrected "—back, so we held it for you."

"Well, I'm here to pick it up."

"That's great. I'll go get it."

Giles spun around and disappeared behind a thick black curtain which separated the front desk area from the mail sorting department. He returned within seconds, carrying a deep plastic tray overflowing with cards and letters. He heaved it onto the counter, causing some of the contents to spill out. Terry picked up one of the letters and read the address. He didn't recognize it.

"Most of it is from the first couple of weeks, when word spread. They've been trickling in ever since, though," said Giles. "And they haven't stopped."

Terry placed the letter back in the tray. "Giles, there was something you wanted to tell me. Do you remember?"

Giles paused for a moment, trying to recall. And then he remembered. "Yes!" Giles yelled out, as if he'd just figured out the winning answer on a TV game show. "There was a package."

"A package?"

"Yes, but I got rid of it."

"Rid of it? Why?"

"'Cuz she asked me to."

Terry knew instantly that he was talking about Hannah.

"She came in that day," began Giles. "In the morning. Asked me if I could return something for her. I asked her what was in it. She said it was cigarettes she'd ordered online. I asked her why she ordered them online and she explained that you wouldn't buy them for her and since she didn't leave the house... well. She asked if I'd return them for her. She'd decided to quit and didn't want them around in case she got tempted. I told her I couldn't. I told her you can't return cigarettes. Said so right on the box. No returns. She told me she didn't want them. She asked if I'd destroy them for her. So that's what I done."

Terry listened intently as he reiterated the story, remembering that he thought he saw her walking down the street that day carrying a package. He was right. It was her.

"She seemed really happy that day. She told me she was going grocery shopping. That she was going to make your favorite dinner."

Tears ran down Terry's cheeks.

"I'm sorry. I shouldn't have told you," Giles said.

"No," said Terry. "I'm glad you did. I'm glad she was happy. At least for that day."

He grabbed the tray of letters from the counter and began to leave.

"Are you coming back?" asked Giles. "'Cuz if you're not, I'm gonna need that container. It's government property." He regretted the words as soon as they left his mouth. "Actually, don't worry about it. I won't tell anyone."

"I'll be back. Just as soon as I'm done reading these. Gonna check into a motel tonight. I'll see you in the morning."

Giles smiled.

Terry nodded politely. He didn't really feel like smiling back.

***

After leaving the post office, Terry found a cheap motel room with a neon flashing light similar to the one outside Hardware California. After checking in, he peeled off his clothes and took a long shower. He watched, head bowed, as the soap slid haphazardly along the crevices of his scars. It was the first time he allowed himself to really see them. Acknowledge them. He had avoided looking at them for over a year.

After a half an hour, he shut off the water, grabbed the flimsy towel off the hook near the shower, and dried off. Then he stood in front of the mirror and examined his body. The scars were a part of him now. He turned around to check out the area of his buttocks where they had "borrowed" some extra skin. His doctors called it an "autograft" because it was taken from another area of his body. This was the safest way, he was told, since other types of donor skin could be rejected by his body.

That was the worst part. He had to spoil another area of his body, as if his disfigured chest wasn't bad enough. Renee hadn't seen his ass yet. He wondered if she'd be turned off. And then he remembered the kind of person she was and he knew, instinctively, that it wouldn't matter to her. In fact, she'd probably make some silly joke about it. And maybe he'd laugh this time.

He wrapped the towel around his torso and then turned on the TV. It was tuned to the station Hannah used to be obsessed with—twenty-four hour news. Bad news. Never good news. He quickly switched it off.

He approached the bed and sat down next to the container spilling over with letters. He reached in and grabbed one. It smelled of perfume. He quickly ripped it open and began to read. It was from a woman he'd never met. She introduced herself as Maggie. She said she heard about what happened and wanted to be there for him. If he should so desire, she left her number.

Please God, he said to himself, *Let them get better than this.*

He began to read another. This one was better. As was the one that followed. And the next.

But it was the seventh letter he opened that really caught his attention. It was from the minister who officiated the funeral proceedings. Terry wasn't able to attend the funeral. He'd been in the hospital recovering. But even if he hadn't been being treated, he still wouldn't have gone. Couldn't have gone. The pain was too great. He was out of his mind with grief and despair and going to the funeral would have been out of the question. Who in their right mind would subject themselves to the prolongation of grief through the process of a meaningless ritual?

But the minister thought otherwise. His letter read:

Dear Mr. Boyle:

We missed you at the funeral, but due to the nature and extent of your injuries, your absence was completely understandable. Had you been there, I believe it would have allowed you to see and feel the outpouring of love this community has for your family. The church was packed with mourners who came to pay their last respects. People often wonder why funerals are important. I believe they are very important because they allow us to face our grief head on and not hide from the reality that death is an inevitable part of life, even tragic deaths. If we don't go, our brains can trick us into thinking that our loved ones are not really dead—that they have merely gone away, perhaps to return one day. We can go on allowing ourselves to believe that the death never occurred. I hope, in time, you'll be able to visit their graves. Even though their souls now belong to the heavens, I urge you to come visit them at the cemetery. Yes, it'll be difficult, but grief is a part of life. And in order to move on, we must face it. If you ever need to talk, please call me. Yours in Christ, Reverend Tony.

After reading the letter, Terry lay back on the bed, emotionally drained, and fell into a deep sleep.

While he was sleeping, he had a dream.

In it, Miranda and Hannah were lying together in a bed of vibrant wildflowers. Hannah was stroking Miranda's hair as Miranda read aloud to her.

"And in a blinding flash," Miranda read as she turned the last page, "the sun returned to the sky. A new day had begun."

Then she rested her head on her mother's lap and said with finality, "The End."

***

The next day, Terry went to visit the graveyard.

They shared a tombstone. Hannah's mother had picked it out. He looked at the dates etched in stone, dates which constituted the brief time frame of their lives—the day their lives began and the day they ended. He wondered what people would think years from now, long after everyone was gone who knew of the tragedy. Would they wonder why they died on the same day? Would they feel sad thinking about what must have happened? Would they wonder why the father lived?

Why the father lived?

Terry thought about this. He had *lived*. He was alive.

***

The parking lot was full of cars, so Terry had to park on the street.

As he approached the entrance of the hardware store, he spotted a hand-made banner above the door which read, *Grand Re-Opening*. And underneath it, the sign—

Hardware California. She didn't get rid of it, after all. It was as neon and bright as ever, blinking off and on, shining as if it was brand new. The sign was there to stay.

And so was he.

THE END

About Bernie Van De Yacht

Originally from Green Bay, Wisconsin, Bernie Van De Yacht is the youngest of thirteen children. He is a screenwriter, director, casting director and co-partner in ProADR Looping. He lives in Glendale, California, with his wife and two sons. *A Man Walks Into a Hardware Store* is his first novel.

Acknowledgments

First and foremost, I'd like to thank my business partner and longtime friend, ML Gemmill. ML and I share many of the same qualities—a strong work ethic, a restless need for creative expression, a strict adherence to The Golden Rule, and an unflappable faith in a higher power. Without her steadfast encouragement and guidance, this book would have never been written.

A heartfelt and humble thanks to my publisher, Solstice Publishing, for their belief and support of this novel, specifically Melissa Miller, Kate Collins, and K.C. Sprayberry.

A load of gratitude to Leslie Lang, Libby Slate, Donna, Celine, and Sophie Thormann, Stephen Jared, Renee Albert, Larry Czerwonka, Rick Dinger, William Cole, Chuck Powers, Lora Baldwin, Erin DiGennaro and again, ML Gemmill, for their eleventh hour suggestions and notes.

A nostalgic thank you to Elizabeth H. Scholten, the first published author from Green Bay, Wisconsin, for inspiring me to put pen to paper all those years ago.

Thank you, Harper Lee, for creating a masterpiece right out of the gate and inspiring a generation of writers. And thank you to all the writers who exist or existed, both published and un- published. We all know how hard, and sometimes lonely, it is to do what we do. But our reward comes when we create that one simple sentence or phrase assembled from the vast amount of words at our disposal that perfectly encapsulates our intent.

I'd like to thank Earl Hamner, Jr., for creating the character of John-Boy Walton. In doing so, you gave a young boy growing up on a small farm in rural Wisconsin an identifiable role model to emulate.

A special thank you to my eighth-grade teacher, Ms. Connie Haack, who once wrote on one of my assignments, "Bernie, you're my first 'writer'!" Your words had a profound impact on me and I wanted you to know that— wherever you are.

And on that note, thank you to all my teachers and professors throughout the years who've cultivated my creative process. You are all heroes to me.

For all my friends, both near and far, old and new, lost and found—you have made me a very successful man. For, as Clarence Odbody: Angel Second Class, wrote to George Bailey at the conclusion of It's a Wonderful Life— "no man is a failure who has friends."

Thank you to my late parents, Bernard and Violetta Van De Yacht, for teaching me right from wrong, and clearly delineating which was which.

Thank you to all of my brothers and sisters—Bill, Leo,

Bob, Diane, Ken, Nick, Gery, Mary-Ann, Kevin, Debbie, Dawn, and Donna, and to their spouses and their children and their children's children. I can't begin to express how much I love and appreciate your support and encouragement throughout the years. You make it easy to come home again.

I am very blessed to have married into my wife's family. Thank you for always making me feel like one of your own.

And finally, thank you to my wife, Valerie, and my sons, Janssen and Joseph. I would say, "You complete me," but I'd never steal another author's words. Thank you, Cameron Crowe. You summed up in three words the perfect way to describe the contentment one feels when those you love bring everything full circle and fill in all the gaps.

But, then again, that's what writers do.

69517187R00121

Made in the USA
Lexington, KY
01 November 2017